BADGE
OF
HONOR

Books by Susan Marlow

Circle C Beginnings
Andi's Pony Trouble
Andi's Indian Summer
Andi's Scary School Days
Andi's Fair Surprise
Andi's Lonely Little Foal
Andi's Circle C Christmas

Circle C Stepping Stones
Andi Saddles Up
Andi Under the Big Top
Andi Lassos Trouble
Andi to the Rescue
Andi Dreams of Gold
Andi Far from Home

Circle C Adventures
Andrea Carter and the Long Ride Home
Andrea Carter and the Dangerous Decision
Andrea Carter and the Family Secret
Andrea Carter and the San Francisco Smugglers
Andrea Carter and the Trouble with Treasure
Andrea Carter and the Price of Truth

Circle C Milestones
Thick as Thieves
Heartbreak Trail
The Last Ride
Courageous Love
Yosemite at Last: And Other Tales from Memory Creek Ranch
Stranger in the Glade: And More Tales from Memory Creek Ranch

Goldtown Beginnings
Jem Strikes Gold
Jem's Frog Fiasco
Jem and the Mystery Thief
Jem Digs Up Trouble
Jem and the Golden Reward
Jem's Wild Winter

Goldtown Adventures
Badge of Honor
Tunnel of Gold
Canyon of Danger
River of Peril

GOLDTOWN ADVENTURES #1

BADGE OF HONOR

SUSAN K. MARLOW

KREGEL
PUBLICATIONS

Badge of Honor
© 2012 by Susan K. Marlow

Illustrations © 2012 by Melissa McConnell

Published by Kregel Publications, a division of Kregel Inc., 2450 Oak Industrial Dr. NE, Grand Rapids, MI 49505.

ISBN 978-0-8254-4294-0

Printed in the United States of America
23 24 25 26 / 8 7 6 5

Contents

⊰ CHAPTER 1 ⊱

Spring Rush

GOLDTOWN, CALIFORNIA, 1864

Standing knee-deep in an icy mountain creek was *not* the way twelve-year-old Jem Coulter planned to welcome spring this year. But when the clouds parted and the sun came out just in time for the noon recess, he had no choice. His legs took off, and his body was obliged to follow.

Jem didn't bother to run back to the ranch for his gold pan. He ducked around the corner of the crumbling, red-brick schoolhouse and headed for his gold claim at a fast trot.

Gold claim, ha! Jem thought with a laugh. A "claim" maybe, but he had never found enough gold in the small strip of land along Cripple Creek to do justice to the word *gold.*

Dirt claim, he quickly amended. The Coulter Family dirt claim. *If I had a nickel for every bucket of dirt I've washed from that claim, I'd be rich. So would Pa.* Jem lost his grin. *Then maybe Pa could have afforded a doctor for Mama, and maybe she would still be alive.*

Jem sighed. Had it really been four whole years since she'd died? If only—

7

"Hey, Jem, wait for me!" a familiar voice sliced into Jem's daydreaming. The *clomp, clomp, clomp* of his ten-year-old sister's high-top shoes brought her alongside him. She snatched at his shirt sleeve and panted. "Slow down, will ya?"

Jem stopped. He shook free of her grasp and groaned. "Roasted rattlesnakes, Ellie! Where do you think *you're* going?"

Ellie's hazel eyes opened wide. "Why, I'm coming with you, of course." She gave him a sly grin. "I know just where you're off to. And if you think you can get first claim to any gold washing down from the spring run-off, well"—she brushed aside a short, auburn braid—"think again."

"Swell," Jem grunted. "Now, instead of Pa skinning me for playing hooky, he'll give me double for dragging you along. You get back to school, ya hear?"

Ellie folded her arms across her chest and scowled. She made no move to obey her big brother.

Jem scowled back. *Sisters! What a bothersome lot!*

It wouldn't be so bad if Ellie acted like other girls her age in Goldtown. Why couldn't she content herself with dressing paper dolls, going to tea parties, and jumping rope? But no, Ellie was always in the thick of things. If Jem climbed a tree, Ellie climbed a taller tree. If he found three flakes of gold, Ellie shivered in the creek until her gold pan held four flakes.

It's downright . . . Jem stopped this train of thought. If truth be told, his sister was more dependable and loyal than any of Jem's friends. And she never, *ever* tattled on him.

"Oh, all right," Jem growled and yanked one of Ellie's scraggly pigtails. "You can come."

Even without his say-so, Ellie would have tagged along, but it made Jem feel in charge when he gave his brotherly permission. "You can catch frogs. I've got a big order to deliver to the café. Mr. Sims is counting on me. He wants to advertise the first frog legs of the season."

Jem turned and took off running again.

Ellie easily kept up. She jogged alongside her brother for a minute, then asked, "At what rate of payment?"

"Huh?" Jem slowed just a hint. He squinted at her in confusion.

"At what rate of payment?" Ellie repeated. "I heard some fella from back East say that the other day. It's city talk for 'How much are you gonna pay me for the frogs?'"

Jem didn't answer. They had reached Cripple Creek and were picking their way through dozens of staked-out gold claims. Most of the claims lay abandoned, pock-marked with holes of all sizes, where prospectors had dug into the ground and the hillsides, hoping to find a rich vein of gold.

To Jem's knowledge, nobody ever had. Found a rich vein of gold, that is.

Most of the gold that had given the town its name and brought it to life fifteen years ago came out of the creek. The placer gold washed down from the mother lode somewhere deep in the heart of the Sierra Nevada, mixed in with the dirt and snow.

The mountains rose sharply in the east, snowcapped and glistening in the spring sunshine. Jem pointed, the frogs momentarily forgotten. "Look, Ellie. There's enough gold up there to make every man, woman, and child in Goldtown rich as King Midas." He sighed. If only more of it would wash downstream and into his gold pan!

Ellie shaded her eyes and looked up.

"At least, that's what Strike says," Jem added.

"Maybelle Sterling says that old man is crazy as a loon," Ellie remarked. She jumped over a large hole in the ground and scrambled across a pile of old diggings. "For all his talk about how to find gold, Strike's the poorest miner I know. He never even changes his clothes."

"He likes those clothes," Jem said, rushing to his friend's

defense. "And don't let that little snip Maybelle tease you. Strike's not crazy, just a little . . . well . . . peculiar."

The small, grizzled prospector was forever wandering up and down the gold fields, scraping together a meager living. His donkey, Canary, carried his provisions and the most important tools of all: gold pans, picks, and shovels. Strike knew the diggings around Goldtown like the back of his hand.

"If it wasn't for him, Pa and Ma would never have learned a thing about how to work a gold claim," Jem reminded Ellie. "They would've starved to death without him. Why, Strike's closer to us than kinfolk!" He paused. "I betcha he strikes it rich some day. That'll show everybody, and—"

"Yoo-hoo, Strike! Found any color?"

Ellie's shout brought Jem around. Had she even been listening to him? As usual, probably not.

Strike-it-rich Sam squatted in the creek next to the Coulter claim, peering into a beat-up gold pan. Water swirled around the ankles of his knee-high boots. One suspender hung off the shoulder of his once-red flannel shirt. Long, gray-streaked hair blew around his face, barely held in place by a battered slouch hat.

At Ellie's shout, he shook the gravel out of his pan and lifted it in greeting. His other hand held a steaming cup of the prospector's special brew.

"Howdy, young'uns," Strike hollered. A smile split his dirt-encrusted beard. "Nope, no color yet. But the coffee's boilin'. Biscuits are hot. Help yerself."

He nodded toward a small fire on the creek bank nearby. A tin bucket sat over the flames, simmering. Three rock-hard, black-bottomed lumps of cooked dough rested in a shallow frying pan next to the fire.

Jem walked over and gave the biscuits a passing glance. Then he peeked into the pot. A dark, thick liquid bubbled.

He cringed. "Thanks, Strike, but we brought our own dinner." He held up his tin lunch pail to prove it.

"I want coffee," Ellie said, taking a step forward.

Jem yanked her back and whispered, "It's terrible coffee, and you're not having any."

Strike might call his concoction coffee, but after one scorching, bitter taste two years ago, Jem knew better than to call it coffee. Tree-bark brew maybe, with a bit of creek mud thrown in for color, but definitely not coffee.

Ellie let it go. She wandered over to a scruffy burro that *hee-hawed* at her approach. She scratched him on his head, just between his long ears. "Howdy, Canary."

The donkey closed his eyes in sleepy pleasure, but he could just as easily have reached out and nipped Ellie. Canary was not the most reliable or easygoing animal in the gold fields.

Jem did not share Ellie's love for the stubborn critter. "Get away from him before he kicks you," he told her. "Come get some dinner." When she sat down beside Jem on a pile of rocks, he tore a chunk of bread in half and handed it to her. "You didn't think to bring along *your* lunch pail, did you? We're gonna be mighty hungry by suppertime."

Ellie shrugged. "I didn't want to go back for it. Miss Cheney might've caught me sneaking off."

A wrinkled, over-wintered apple completed their scanty meal. Jem let Ellie have the final bite and watched her take the core to Canary. Then he stood up and looked around. Four or five hardy souls were hunkered down along both sides of the stream a little distance away, washing their diggings. "Looks like we've pretty much got this place to ourselves today," he said.

Strike had left the creek and was pouring himself another cup of the sludge he called coffee. He reached into a pack on the ground, pulled out a spare gold pan, and tossed it to Jem.

"You'll find out in a hurry why that's so. Wade in and see how long you last." He chuckled.

Jem caught the pan and stepped into the creek. Even through his boots he felt the icy chill of melted snow coming down from the high country. He clamped his jaw shut against the shock.

Freezing near to death will be worth it if I can strike it rich this afternoon. I'd be happy to pan even an ounce—just a thumb-sized gold nugget—please! Jem realized with a sharp pang that his thoughts had slid effortlessly into a prayer. *We need the money, God. An ounce or two of gold would go a long way toward getting ourselves a decent bull for the herd.*

Jem knew why his father had bought the run-down ranch three years ago—if owning a couple dozen head of cattle could even be *called* ranching. It was Matt Coulter's desperate attempt to make a living in a town that no longer lived up to its name, Goldtown. The family had managed to wash enough gold to scrape by in the early years. But their claim had never been a rich strike, not like other miners in the area.

Now the gold was gone—most of it, anyway. The new Midas mine was making an attempt at hard-rock mining underground, but the easy-to-find placer gold above ground was pretty much played out.

"Maybe this spring will be different," Jem told himself between chattering teeth. He scraped a double handful of creek gravel into his pan. "All that melting snow might carry a bit of color mixed in with the dirt."

Jem's excitement rose a notch at the possibility. It was no secret Pa thought their claim was nothing more than a worthless piece of dirt. Jem and Ellie were allowed to fool around out here during their free time, but Pa no longer took it seriously.

"But if I find gold this spring, all that will change!" Jem said. Ideas rushed through his head. "It would prove our claim *isn't* played out. Then Pa wouldn't have to work so hard on the ranch. Ellie could have a new dress. I could quit my frog and firewood businesses. All I need is one big nugget and—"

Strike's sudden *whoop* made Jem jump a foot. A yell like that from the old miner could mean only one thing—Strike-it-rich Sam had struck it rich.

⊰ CHAPTER 2 ⊱

Caught in the Act

Jem dropped his gold pan, snatched it up again before it could float away, and sloshed his way over to Strike. By the time he crowded around the prospector, Ellie was there too, eyes popping and mouth hanging open.

"What didja find, Strike?" she asked, tugging on his shirt sleeve. "How big? Lemme see!"

Jem's heart raced. If Strike had washed a large nugget out of the creek bed already, then there was a chance Jem could do the same. A big strike meant school would close early. Miners would line up along the creek bank again, laughing and swapping stories of Goldtown's boom days.

Jem leaned forward. Surely that *whoop* meant his friend had pulled a fist-sized chunk of pure gold from Cripple Creek. It might weigh a pound! Maybe even two pounds. Or perhaps Strike had washed something smaller. Even a thumb-sized nugget was worthy of a hearty yell.

He looked down. Fine sand, small pieces of gravel, and a glint of gold greeted Jem's curious gaze, but no chunks. *Where's the big strike?* He bent closer.

"Get yer shaggy brown head out of my pan," Strike growled with rough affection. "I can't see a blamed thing."

"Doesn't look like there's much *to* see," Jem grouched. *Another hope dashed.* He shivered in the early afternoon sun. "Hang it all, Strike! Why are you whooping over three pieces of gold the size of radish seeds?"

"You'd holler plenty loud if that gold was in *your* pan," Ellie shot back. "I don't see you finding any color."

"That's 'cause I was interrupted by false strike-it-rich claims!"

"There ain't nothin' false about it, boy," Strike said. Carefully, he dug into his back pocket and pulled out a small leather pouch. It was limp—worn-out from much handling— and empty. "Gold is gold, whether it's gold dust, radish-seed nuggets, or a hunk big enough for a doorstop."

He handed the pouch to Ellie, who quickly pulled the mouth of the small sack open. Using tweezers from another pocket, Strike fished the tiny bits of gold from his pan and dropped them in his pouch.

He smiled. "First gold of 1864. I 'spect this will be a good year for me." He took the now-closed leather bag from Ellie and stuffed it back into his pocket.

"You say that every year," Jem muttered, too low for his friend to hear. Strike-it-rich Sam had never, *ever* struck it rich. His small pouch was never more than half full. *Why did I think it would be different this year?*

He splashed back to his claim with a sigh. "I guess I better not quit my other jobs just yet." Turning to Ellie, he shouted, "Get the lunch pail and go after those frogs!"

Ellie grinned at him from the creek bank. "At what rate of payment, Jem?"

Jem let out a frustrated breath. *Sisters! What a bothersome lot!*

It took a bit of haggling, but Ellie finally agreed to catch frogs for a penny apiece. He quickly shook her hand to seal the bargain and watched her skip off toward the boggy swamp a hundred yards up the creek. A warm spring fed the marsh, and Jem had high hopes that some of the hoppers had come out of hibernation early. Mr. Sims would buy as many as Jem could deliver.

"Ellie will probably have better luck catching frogs than I'll have panning gold," Jem told Strike. "Too bad gold nuggets don't multiply like frogs do."

Strike burst out laughing, as if Jem had told a funny joke. Jem scowled. He didn't think it was all that funny. His feet were numb inside his boots from crouching in the creek, and his hands shook with cold. He struggled to fill his gold pan with creek mud and gravel.

"I d-don't see how you do it," Jem said, teeth chattering. "You're n-not even shivering. You look as warm as a lizard sunning itself on a rock. Aren't you c-cold?"

"We-lll . . ." Strike dragged the word out while he peered into his pan. "I reckon not. I don't pay no never-mind to heat or cold. My hide's pert-near as tough as a little ol' lizard's."

He took out his tweezers and poked around in his pan. "We-lll, lookee here. What d'ya know? Another one of them radish-seed gold specks. I reckon a pouch full of 'em would make a good-sized stake." He dropped the tiny piece of gold in with the others. Then he winked at Jem.

Jem flushed. As much as he hated to admit it, Strike and Ellie were right: gold was gold, no matter how big or small the strike. "I guess I'd whoop plenty loud if I found gold in my pan this afternoon," he said. "I'd probably forget how cold I am too."

Too chilled to swirl his pan without losing the entire

load—possible gold and all—Jem stepped out of the creek and hovered over the fire. He was tempted to take a swallow of Strike's coffee to warm his insides but thought better of it.

When his hands had thawed, Jem picked up a shovel and returned to the creek. He stood alongside the swirling water and scooped a little of the creek bank into his pan. Sometimes, gold flecks became lodged in the dirt between plant roots.

Jem squatted on the bank and added water. He worked his load of dirt and tried to enjoy the sounds of the creek splashing past him and the swishing of rocks and water against his pan. Unfortunately, the constant *clang, clang, clang* of the Midas mine's new stamp mill overshadowed the creek noises. The clamor of the ore-crushing machine could be heard miles away.

Jem wished there was another way to separate gold from rock besides smashing it. But the underground veins of quartz did not give up their gold easily. Crushing the rocks into coarse sand was the first step in separating the precious treasure. "Give me a gold pan and a quiet stream any day," he muttered.

Jem ignored the banging the best he could and concentrated on the task at hand. It was long, boring work that required a good deal of patience. Jem could muster up a decent share of patience, at least when it paid off.

And it paid off today.

The *whoop* Jem let out sounded identical to Strike's whoop from an hour before. "I hit color! It's no radish seed either. It's an honest-to-goodness real gold nugget!"

The prospector waded over to Jem and clapped him on the back. "Show me, partner."

The thrill of finding color sent a warm rush through Jem, as did the sound of Strike calling him "partner." Now that Pa couldn't be bothered teaming up with the old miner, Jem was happy to take his place.

He fished around in his pan, then held up a gold nugget the size of a large corn kernel.

Strike whistled, long and low. "Nice work, young fella. Didn't I say this was gonna be a good year?"

Jem nodded. "This was worth playing hooky from school for. Betcha there's more where that came from."

Before Jem could try his luck a second time, he spotted a small figure running alongside the bank on the opposite side of the creek. It was Ellie. "I heard you hollering," she shouted at the top of her lungs. "Did you strike it rich?"

"Come and see."

In a flash, Ellie pulled off her shoes and stockings, stuffed everything under her arm, and picked up the pail of frogs. She slammed the lid firmly in place, then stepped into the icy creek. It was slippery going over the sharp rocks, but Ellie managed to make it across without getting dunked.

"It's cold!" she exclaimed.

"How did you get across the first time?" Jem wanted to know.

"I found a place to cross upstream, where I didn't have to take off my shoes." She dropped her stockings, shoes, and the pail on the ground. "Let me see your gold."

Jem opened his hand and let Ellie admire his gold nugget. When her eyes opened to twice their normal size, he knew she was properly impressed.

"Do you reckon there's more?" she asked.

Jem grinned. "I plan to find out. Betcha there's"—his eyebrows shot up—"hey, where are you going?"

Ellie had snatched up the gold pan and was stepping back into the creek. "Where do you think?"

"It's too cold to wade barefoot," Jem told her, slipping his precious nugget into his pocket. It would be safe there until he put it in his gold pouch at home. "Get out of that water and put your shoes back on."

Ellie paid no attention. Like the experienced little miner she was, she scooped up a load of dirt and gravel and began the long, slow process of panning for gold. "If you found a nugget, I can too."

Jem slapped a hand against his forehead. "Why don't you ever do what I tell you, Ellie? Get outta there or I'll drag you out. The creek's nothin' but melted snow."

"Not until I find myself a nugget," Ellie insisted.

Jem took a step toward the creek. The last thing he wanted was a wrestling match with his spunky little sister. But he couldn't let her catch a chill and get sick. He turned to Strike in desperation. "Strike, can you give me a hand pulling Ellie out—"

"Ellianna, get out of the creek."

Jem froze.

Ellie froze too, but only for a second. She scrambled out of the water and over the bank like a startled jackrabbit. Her gold pan clattered to the ground. She skidded to a stop next to Jem, breathing hard and shaking with cold—or fear. Jem didn't know which. Probably a little of both.

Jem slowly turned and faced the tall, dark-haired man standing on a pile of old diggings a stone's throw away. His vest and pants were covered with dirt; his shirt was dark with sweat. It looked like he'd been working hard before . . .

Before coming out here, Jem thought in dismay. Suddenly, all plans of striking it rich flew from Jem's head. He forgot how cold he was or how irritated he was at Ellie. Only one thought went round and round in his mind.

Pa's gonna skin me alive for playing hooky!

⊰ CHAPTER 3 ⊱

Goldtown

"Good afternoon, Jeremiah," Matt Coulter said, pushing back his wide-brimmed hat. He was not smiling. "What are you two doing this fine spring day?"

Jem knew his father didn't really expect an answer. Pa could look around and see that his children were not in school, where they were supposed to be. And when he started using their full names, Jem knew he and Ellie were in trouble.

Big trouble.

Suddenly, finding a gold nugget was *not* worth playing hooky from school.

"H-howdy, Pa," Jem managed to get out. "What are you doing here?" *Dumb question.*

"Jem hit color!" Ellie piped up. "It's real pretty." She elbowed her brother. "Show him."

Jem dug in his trouser pocket for the gold and scurried over to show off his treasure.

Pa took the nugget. He studied it for a full minute, while Jem stared at the ground. He wished his father would say, "Good strike" or "That's a beauty" or "Nice start." Maybe even let out a low whistle. But he didn't.

Pa handed the gold nugget to Jem without a word. Then

Goldtown

he turned to Ellie. "Put your shoes and socks on, young lady. You and your brother are going back to school."

Ellie flopped to the ground and began pulling the long, black woolen stockings over her wet feet and legs.

"But Pa!" Jem stuffed the nugget back in his pocket. "School's nearly out. Wouldn't you rather—" He stopped talking. His gaze was riveted on a dusty, metal *something* fastened to his father's vest. Jem peered closer. "What's that thing on your vest?"

Ellie paused with one shoe in her hand. "What thing?"

Pa looked down. "You mean this?" He rubbed the dirt away to reveal a shiny, six-pointed silver star. Clean now, it glistened in the sun. "It's a sheriff's badge, Jem," he explained, smiling. "Haven't you ever seen one before?"

Jem nodded, stunned. *Sure, I've seen one. I just never figured to see one on my pa.* What did Goldtown need a sheriff for, anyway? The miners' court had worked fine for years and years. Whose terrible idea was this? Surely not Pa's!

"The mayor and town council have been talking for months about hiring a sheriff," Pa said. "This morning they hired me to be the first sheriff of Goldtown."

"But *why?*" Jem asked when he found his tongue. "And what about the ranch? Who's going to run it if you're off breaking up fights and arresting claim jumpers and . . ." His voice trailed off. *And maybe getting shot.* No, Pa's accepting the job as sheriff of rough-and-tumble Goldtown, California, was *not* a good idea.

"Most folks in Goldtown wear more than one hat," Pa said. "Pappy Baxter runs the livery, prospects, and does a fine job as barber on Saturday nights. I can sheriff and run the ranch." Then he frowned. "But I didn't hike all the way out here to talk about my new job. You two are returning to school for the rest of the day. I believe Miss Cheney has a couple of corners already picked out."

Ellie finished putting on her shoes and snatched up the bucket of frogs. Her teeth were chattering. "I hope she puts me in the corner by the stove." She didn't say anything about Pa's new badge.

Jem rolled his eyes. "I told you to stay out of that creek, but—"

"Enough," Pa said. "Let's go." He waved a brief greeting to Strike. "Howdy, Strike."

The prospector waved back. "I see they finally pinned a star on you, boy. Hope it don't weigh you down too much. But if this gold camp's gotta have a lawman, I reckon yer the best man for the job. Got time for coffee?"

Pa shook his head. "I have to get these two rascals back to town so the schoolmarm can lick 'em good."

Strike nodded. "Yer first official act as sheriff, eh? Roundin' up yer truant kids. Folks'll see the humor in that." He slapped his knee and cackled. "Yesiree, they surely will."

Jem felt two hot spots grow on his cheeks. He and Ellie exchanged glum looks.

Yep, Pa taking the job as sheriff is a really bad idea, any way you look at.

As they hiked back to town, Jem wanted nothing more than to fire questions at Pa about his new job. He wanted to beg him to give the star back to Mayor Gordon and the town council. *Why would Pa accept such a dangerous job?* But Jem didn't get a chance to ask even one question. Pa was doing all the talking.

"I don't have time to be running after you kids," Pa said with a heavy sigh. "Now that spring's here, I need every bit of daylight to get things up and running on the ranch." He paused. "That is, if we all want to go on eating. And now, with my extra duties . . ." He let the rest go unsaid.

Jem felt a stab of guilt. "I'm sorry, Pa. I didn't plan on playing hooky. It just happened. The sun was shining and . . ." His voice trailed off at his father's disappointed look.

"Nothing 'just happens,' Jeremiah, and you know it. And I'm not done talking, so put a hand over your mouth and let me finish."

"Yes, sir." He peeked at Ellie. Her eyes looked huge and scared. Jem knew she didn't like being scolded any more than he did.

"I especially didn't like being pulled away from my very first day as sheriff," Pa was saying. "I was wrestling Nine Toes out of the newest mining hole he'd dug in the middle of the street, when the Sterling boy ran up. He took great pleasure in telling me—in front of half the town—that Miss Cheney wanted to see me right away, on account of *my children were missing from the schoolroom!*"

Jem winced at his father's raised voice. Pa hardly ever yelled, at least not like some men Jem knew. He'd heard plenty of shouting and cussing when he passed the saloons in town. He was mighty glad his father was "slow to anger" like the Good Book said.

But Pa occasionally raised his voice when he had a good reason. Like if an ornery steer broke through a fence. Or a wolf went after the calves. Or—Jem swallowed—like now, when his father had to deal with the snooty rich folks from up on Belle Hill.

"Miss Cheney sent Will Sterling to fetch you?" Jem asked, astonished.

"The little weasel," Ellie huffed. "Jem, you oughta pound him right into the—"

"Ellianna."

At Pa's warning, Ellie's mouth snapped shut.

Jem agreed with Ellie but said nothing. He was thinking plenty, however. Didn't Miss Cheney have better sense than to give the mine owner's son a chance to gloat over somebody else's troubles?

"Yes," Pa said in a tired voice, "she sent him. When I

23

finally got around to seeing Miss Cheney, she gave me an earful." He shook his head. "Sometimes, Son, I wonder what goes on in your head. You're older. You need to watch out for your sister, not drag her into trouble with you."

"Pa!" Ellie came to a standstill. "Jem did *not* drag me into anything. I saw him take off and knew right where he was going. It's not Jem's fault. Don't punish him on my account."

"That's probably true enough," Pa agreed, "but I don't need your help deciding my punishments. Now, let's get a move on."

Through the scattered oak and pine trees lining the well-worn path, the outlying buildings of Goldtown came into view. Jem dreaded returning to school. It was no fun to stand in a corner while the whole class snickered at you from behind their hands. Miss Cheney would make him copy lines too. One hundred, most likely.

He reached in his pocket and curled his fingers around his nugget. *At least I have this.*

They were picking their way along the main street of Goldtown now. Mud squished around Jem's boots and splattered his damp britches. Ellie ran ahead, her shoes making *slop, slop, slop* sounds. With a leap, she landed on the wooden sidewalk. It was just as muddy, but at least it was solid ground.

Jem stepped up on the boardwalk after her. "Pa, why don't you come out and work the claim with us? You saw my nugget. There's gotta be more. We could—"

"That sorry claim has never produced enough gold to do more than help us scrape by," Pa reminded Jem. "Why do you think I bought the ranch? After ten years of washing diggings, I'm worn out. There's no future in small, placer gold claims anymore. The future is up there."

Pa pointed to a hill that rose beyond the buildings across the street. It was the site of the Midas mine, and all eyes in

Goldtown were on it. "But I'd rather starve as a rancher above ground than sweat and suffocate below it," he said, dropping his arm to his side.

Jem opened his mouth to argue, but Pa held up his hand. "I know you love to prospect, Jem, and I understand." He grinned at Jem's astonished look. "Yes, I really do understand. But it's over for me, and until school's out this term, it's over for you too." He turned to Ellie. "And you."

Jem caught his breath. He and Ellie exchanged horrified looks. School would not be out until the middle of May—more than a month from now!

Punishment number one.

"Now, back to school with you," Pa said.

Jem glanced down Main Street. He couldn't see the schoolhouse. It was two streets over, sandwiched between the firehouse and the Methodist church. It was an ugly brick building—more like a prison than a school—but after the fire of 1857, nearly every building in town had been rebuilt in brick.

A few buildings along Main Street had survived the fire. One was the Black Skillet café. As the Coulter family passed the establishment, a large, round man with a handlebar moustache and a dingy white apron joined them on the wooden sidewalk.

He wiped his hands on his apron and said, "I'll be needin' those frogs you promised me, Jem. Double quick."

Ellie held up the pail and smiled brightly at the café owner. "I got 'em right here, Mr. Sims."

Mr. Sims took the lunch pail. "Let's see what you got." He lifted the lid and did a quick count. A slight frown creased his forehead. "I count six hoppers, kids. It's a start, but I need a good many more than this."

"Sorry, Sims," Pa broke in. "Jem's going to be too busy for a while to keep you supplied."

Jem's heart sank. He was the top frog-leg supplier in all of Goldtown. If the other boys caught wind of this, he could lose Mr. Sims as a customer.

Pa pointed to Jem's lunch pail. "Keep the frogs, Sims. No charge. Jem will be by later to pick up his pail. He needs it for school tomorrow." The men shook hands, Sims grinning like a fox in a henhouse. Pa's smile was nearly as wide.

Jem groaned. *Punishment number two.*

The wooden sidewalk stretched two more blocks before the Coulters had to turn the corner to the school. Along this bustling portion of Goldtown, dozens of merchants, peddlers, Chinese laundrymen, and miners lingered. The family threaded their way through the crowd. Jem knew a few of these folks, but his father seemed to know them all. Most gave the new sheriff hearty congratulations when they saw his silver badge.

When they reached the Big Strike saloon, Mr. Tobias, the bartender, was sweeping mud off the boardwalk. He saw Jem, paused, and leaned on his broom. "Say, young fella. Where's my sawdust? The floor inside's mostly bare—and muddier than a pig's wallow from all the rain we've had."

"It's all bagged up, sir," Jem quickly assured the man. "I can bring the sacks by this evening, if Pa says so." Jem gave his father a pleading look.

Pa nodded. But he wasn't smiling.

"Good enough," Mr. Tobias agreed, giving the walkway a final swipe with his broom. "See you then."

"You may fill Toby's order this time, since you promised him," Pa said as they walked on. "But after today he'll have to get his sawdust from one of the other boys. I didn't realize you were selling to the saloons."

"Just to the Big Strike," Jem explained in a hurry. "I can't give it up. Mr. Tobias pays good, Pa. Real good."

"No. You will not do business with a saloon."

Jem bristled. "Is it because you're the sheriff now, and I gotta set a good—"

"No," Pa interrupted with a frown. "It's because it's a dirty, ungodly place. You'll just have to content yourself with your firewood customers and selling frog legs to the cafés."

Jem had no choice but to say, "Yes, Pa," but he sighed deeply at the loss of this money-making venture. Bagging up and selling sawdust from the lumberyard was a lot easier than chopping and splitting firewood.

Jem and Ellie were just about to make the turn onto Fremont Street and school, when a familiar pounding and jingling broke through the general hubbub of Goldtown. The weekly stagecoach pulled up to the Wells Fargo Express office to the shout of "Whoa there. Easy now!" from the driver. The four horses snorted, tossed their heads, and slopped around in the mud before coming to a standstill.

"Howdy, Matt!" the driver called from the high seat on top of the coach. "Stick around. The stage brought you somethin' today. A couple of somethin's, actually." Swinging down, he landed in the thick, soupy mud and flung the stagecoach door open.

"Goldtown, folks," he announced. "Boarding house and hotels to the right; saloons and gambling parlors to the left. Post office across the street. Mining supplies one block north.

Stage leaves at seven o'clock sharp tomorrow morning, if you change your mind about staying."

Jem grinned. Walt gave the same speech every time he pulled into town. It didn't matter if the passenger was a Goldtown resident or a fresh face from back East.

A large man dressed in a dark suit and bowler hat stepped out of the stage first. He grimaced when his first step landed in the mud. He quickly crossed to the boardwalk in front of the Express office. When he saw Pa, he offered his hand. "Hello, Matt."

Pa shook it. "Welcome back, Ernest. I hope your business down south went well."

"It did." He reached out and tapped the shiny star. "I see the council finally talked you into accepting the job. Congratulations, Sheriff."

Jem watched the exchange and wondered how his father could speak so nicely to Mr. Sterling, especially after his son had carried tales to Pa from the teacher. He didn't have time to wonder for long, however. A wavering voice suddenly called out from the stage.

"H-hello, Matthew."

Jem and Ellie glanced up as one. The voice belonged to a woman. She stood as still as a statue in the open doorway, staring at Pa with huge, dark eyes. A limp hat hung off the side of her head. Her face was drained of color.

A young boy's face appeared in the window next to her. He glanced at the mud, the crowded boardwalk, and the dozens of buildings lining the street. Then he ducked out of sight.

"I'm here, Matthew," the woman said in a stronger voice. "But never in my wildest dreams did I expect such a God-forsaken place like this mud hole. It's worse than I imagined." She threw her hands over her ears and flinched. "And what is that infernal, banging racket?"

Pa took off his hat and slapped the dirt and mud from his

clothes the best he could. "That's just the stamp mill crushing rocks from the mine, to free up the gold. Might as well get used to it." He grinned and jammed his hat back on his head. "Welcome to Goldtown, big sister."

⊰ CHAPTER 4 ⊱

A Muddy Welcome

Jem's mouth fell open. So did Ellie's. But neither one of
them said a word. Jem continued to stare at the woman—
no, aunt, he corrected himself. He watched her face scrunch
up in a look of confusion, distaste, then weary acceptance.
She took Pa's hand and let him help her from the stagecoach.
She barely came up to his shoulder.

"Come on, Rose," Pa said, nearly picking her up. "Let me
help you . . . one more step. I've got you. There . . . safe at
last." He was wearing a silly smile that told Jem how glad Pa
was to see his older sister after all these years. Matt Coulter
and his new bride had left Boston for the gold fields in '49,
and they had never looked back.

Jem wasn't quite so glad to see his aunt. Ellie didn't look
too happy either. When Pa had read them Aunt Rose's letter
last fall, spring seemed a long way off. There had been plenty
of time to push aside the idea of a strange aunt and a new
cousin coming out West to live with them.

"Expect us sometime next spring," the letter had said. *"Nathan
and I intend to take a steamer around the Horn. They say it takes
six or seven months, barring mishaps or major storms. From San*

A Muddy Welcome

Francisco, we will board a riverboat to Stockton, then take the stage to Goldtown.

"Our lives have turned upside down since dear Frederick was killed in the Battle of Gettysburg this past July. But it will be good to see you, Matthew, after fifteen long years apart. Having kinfolk nearby will surely help my son and me weather this new transition . . ."

The letter had gone on to say how difficult it would be to exchange the refined, bustling city of Boston for a small, rough gold town in the California foothills.

". . . but one must meet hardship with courage," Aunt Rose's letter had finally ended. *"And with Ellen in her grave nearly four years, I know you will welcome my coming to keep house and raise your poor, motherless children."*

Yep, Jem remembered with a sigh, spring had seemed months away last fall. But now? Spring was here, and so were the kinfolk.

"M-mother?"

A quavering voice brought Jem back to the present. His cousin stood in the stage's doorway, looking as bewildered as his mother had only moments before. He was slicked up in city clothes, but his jacket, tie, and knickers were rumpled and dusty. A hank of pale hair peeked out from under the brim of his cap and fell into his eyes. He didn't bother to brush it aside.

"Come along, Nathan," Aunt Rose directed, "and try not to get your shoes muddy. They are your only good pair."

Jem glanced down at his own feet. Mud was a mainstay of Goldtown's winter and spring. Soon enough, the town would be dry as dust in the hot California sun. But Nathan's shoes stood no chance of staying clean today.

Jem laughed. "The only way to keep your feet clean is if you jump *over* the mud."

"That so?" The next instant, Nathan launched himself from the open doorway.

"Nathan, no!" Pa shouted, but it was too late.

31

Jem watched, speechless, as his cousin flew across the muddy gap. Nathan landed on both feet just shy of his goal and sank six inches into the muck. Thick, brown mud splattered everyone standing nearby—Pa, Jem, Ellie, Aunt Rose, and the stage driver.

"Loco young pup," Walt muttered. He wiped a glob of mud from his shirt sleeve and headed for the back of the stage to untie the baggage.

Ellie gasped and swiped at the mud on her dress. "Jem! What did you tell him *that* for?"

Jem felt his cheeks explode in color. "I only meant there's no good way to keep your feet clean around here unless you jump over the mud. I didn't think our cousin would actually make such a tomfool leap—"

A firm hand clapped Jem on the shoulder. "Your tongue is digging your grave, Son," Pa quietly warned.

Jem closed his mouth and surveyed the damage. Nathan had not moved from where he'd landed. He looked as stiff as a scarecrow in a corn field. His face was nearly the color of Strike's red flannel shirt. Muddy specks stood out on his cheeks and forehead like dark freckles.

Aunt Rose appeared dumbstruck at the sight of her son. Her hand covered her mouth, and her eyes were round with shock and dismay.

"That was a bold leap, young fella," Pa said. "But around here it's best to pick your way through the mud a bit more carefully." He waved toward Nathan. "Jem, why don't you give your cousin a hand, since this was your numbskull idea."

While Jem hurried to do as his father asked, Pa turned to Aunt Rose. "I apologize for the welcome, Rosie. This isn't exactly how I wanted you to meet my children. But that's Jeremiah, fishing Nathan out of the mud, and this is Ellianna." He put an arm around his daughter's shoulders and pulled her close. "Say howdy to your Aunt Rose, Ellie."

"Howdy."

Aunt Rose did not return Ellie's greeting. "Land sakes, child! What happened to your hair?"

Jem hauled his cousin up on the boardwalk and held his breath to hear what Ellie would say. If truth be told, he still cringed whenever someone noticed his sister's short, raggedy braids. Ellie could be mighty persistent at times, and long hair was certainly a bother. But Jem never, *ever* should have let Ellie talk him into cutting it off.

A year later, Jem still regretted his decision, and not just because Pa had warmed his backside. The occasional shocked looks and "poor dear" remarks from Goldtown's busybodies often reminded Jem of his mistake. He sure didn't want this new, highfalutin city aunt to give him an earful for a deed long since past.

Ellie smiled. "We Coulters like our hair short, Auntie. Less trouble all the way around." She held up an auburn braid. "One pigtail's a mite longer than the other though. Could you even them up for me sometime?"

Jem let out the breath he'd been holding and flashed his sister a grateful smile.

"I would be happy to do that for you, Ellianna," Aunt Rose said. She turned to her brother and sighed. "It appears I have arrived in good time, Matthew."

A muscle twitched in Pa's jaw. "We haven't done too badly. Jem can cook up a pretty good pot of rabbit stew. However"— he ruffled Ellie's hair to show he was teasing—"this little lady's biscuits could use a bit of help."

"My biscuits are a heap better than Strike's," Ellie shot back. "At least you can bite into them. Strike's pan biscuits are good only for throwing." She looked up at her aunt. "He killed a rattler with a biscuit once. Said it worked near as good as a bullet."

"Strike has worn that story out by now, I'm thinkin'," Pa

said. "It was a baby snake, and he dumped the entire *pan* of biscuits on it."

"Who or what is a 'Strike'?" Aunt Rose asked, frowning.

"A miner friend," Ellie replied at once. "He—"

"Is it true there are rattlesnakes in this part of the country?" Aunt Rose interrupted. She pulled Nathan close to her side and backed up against the wall of the Express office. Her gaze darted to her feet, as if she expected a rattlesnake to strike right through the cracks in the boardwalk.

Jem was eager to assure his aunt that yes, there were plenty of rattlesnakes in the hills and on the ranch—even though he'd killed less than half a dozen in all his twelve years. Maybe such knowledge would keep Nathan in the house, instead of following Ellie and him around.

Before Jem could share his news out loud, the stage driver broke in. "Here's the first of your luggage, ma'am." Walt dragged a large steamer trunk up on the wooden sidewalk and let it drop. "It's a good thing the stage wasn't full this trip, Matt," he said with a laugh. "Your sister's baggage took up near as much room as a couple of paying passengers." He climbed to the top of the stage to untie more luggage.

A few minutes later, a pile of trunks, carpetbags, and battered satchels surrounded the Coulters and their kin. Walt slung the mail pouch over his shoulder, shook his head, and headed for the post office across the street.

Pa shoved his hat back and whistled. Jem and Ellie gawked. How could one grown lady and a half-grown boy own so many belongings?

Jem wanted to ask but—remembering his big mouth earlier—kept his question to himself. Instead he said, "We're definitely going to need the wagon, Pa. Do you want me to run out to the ranch and fetch it?"

Jem's heart pounded as he waited for an answer. His father seemed to be arguing with himself, and Jem could almost read his thoughts. *Help with the relatives? Or drag the kids back to school?* Jem glanced up at the one luxury the town boasted: a small tower clock hauled in from back East two years ago. The time read twenty minutes to four. *School's out at four. It's not worth going back for twenty minutes. Please, Pa!*

Pa sighed. "I reckon it's too late to go back to school now. But tomorrow morning, you and Ellie have an apology to make to Miss Cheney. And you'll accept whatever punishment she hands out. Agreed?"

"Yes, sir!" Jem and Ellie shouted together.

"All right then," Pa said. "Jem, run back to the ranch and hitch up the wagon. We'll need to haul all this baggage and get Aunt Rose and Nathan settled before—"

"Matt! Matt Coulter!"

All three Coulters, along with Aunt Rose and Nathan, whirled at the shout. A man dressed in miners' clothes— filthy and threadbare—came running along the boardwalk. He shoved passersby out of his way and paid no attention to the mean looks and insults he received for his rudeness. He seemed intent only on reaching Pa.

"I was hoping you might be here, meeting the stage," the man said, panting. "If not, I was gonna try your spread." He took big gulps of air. "But by then it probably woulda been too late."

"What would've been too late? What's going on?" Pa grabbed the miner's shoulders. "Tell me, Casey."

No-luck Casey rubbed a hand over his balding scalp and burst out, "It's that blamed knucklehead, Dakota Joe. You know what a temper he's got. He's accusing Frenchy of jumpin' his claim again. They're down at the Big Strike."

"Aw, Casey," Pa said in disgust and backed away. "Dakota and Frenchy go round and round at least once a week over some claim or another. Nothing ever comes of it."

Casey shook his head. "It's different this time, Matt. Frenchy found some others to back him up, and a seedy-looking bunch they are too! New faces. I don't recognize 'em." He drew a deep breath. "And Dakota somehow got hold of an Arkansas toothpick. Sure as shootin', somebody's gonna get cut up real bad."

⤙ CHAPTER 5 ⤚

Trouble

Jem sucked in his breath at No-luck Casey's words. Another fight in Goldtown was nothing new. The miners were always brawling with each other, cursing and hitting. Black eyes and missing teeth were everyday sights. There was plenty of claim jumping too, especially as the easy gold disappeared. Dakota Joe had twice lost a choice plot of pay dirt when he couldn't stand up to better-armed men.

But now it appeared that Dakota was taking matters into his own hands—with a vengeance. An Arkansas toothpick—a long-bladed, evil knife—could easily slice up a man so badly he would bleed to death.

Why are you telling Pa this? Jem wanted to shout. *Pa's a rancher. Or a prospector. He's not the law . . .* His thoughts slid to a standstill as he spotted the new star his father wore. *Wrong. Pa* is *the law now.*

Jem felt Ellie edge up next to him and clutch his arm. He jumped at her touch and tore his attention away from the badge. No-luck Casey was talking a mile a minute.

"Toby down at the Big Strike sent me for you, Matt. He saw you in town earlier. Now that you're wearin' that star, you—"

Pa waved the miner quiet and ran his fingers through

his dark hair. Then he glanced down at his badge. "The timing's mighty inconvenient, what with my sister just arriving. There's no telling how long it'll take to settle this. But"—he looked at Casey—"I reckon I'd best get down there."

Jem sagged inwardly. "Pa? Do you have to meddle in every little miner's squabble, even if you *are* the sheriff? What if they go after you with that knife?"

Pa reached out and took Jem by the shoulders. "A soft answer turns away wrath, Son. That's what Proverbs says. I intend to talk softly, keep both eyes open, and let God do the rest. I don't want to see any of those scoundrels lying dead or cut up on the saloon floor. If Dakota kills Frenchy, he'll hang. I've got to do my job and try to stop this." He squeezed Jem's shoulders in assurance. "Don't worry. I'll be all right."

"Yes, sir," Jem said, but his stomach clenched. How could Pa know for sure he would be all right? *This sheriff business is not safe. Please, God, take care of my pa!*

"I want you to fetch the wagon and bring it to town," Pa instructed. "If I'm not back, ask Josh in the Express office to help you load up the baggage, then you drive everybody out to the ranch. I'll unload the wagon when I get home." He gave Ellie a quick hug. "Mind your brother and your aunt, ya hear?"

"Yes, sir," Ellie whispered. "Please be careful, Pa."

Pa grinned, ruffled Ellie's hair, and winked at her. Then he was gone, running down the wooden sidewalk toward the Big Strike saloon, with No-luck Casey right on his heels.

"Saints preserve us!" Aunt Rose said, fanning herself. "A knife fight in broad daylight. The very idea!"

"Do you suppose . . . I mean . . . do you think I could watch?" Nathan asked. His eyes were bright, eager. He didn't look scared at all.

"You're crazy," Ellie said.

Jem agreed. "You don't know what you're saying, Cousin." Nathan probably wasn't frightened because—most likely—

he'd never seen a for-real, bloody, terrible knife fight. If he had, he would not be so eager to watch another one.

"Nathan Frederick Tyson!" Aunt Rose scolded. "Indeed, you shall not watch such a display." She turned to Jem. "Your father never told me he was sheriff of this gold camp."

Ellie squinted up at Aunt Rose. "That's because he just took the job today. Goldtown's very first sheriff." She did not sound excited.

"I declare!" Aunt Rose exclaimed. "Who broke up these fights before my brother became the law?"

"Nobody, really," Jem said. "Goldtown's always been a rowdy camp. They hold a miners' court if things get too bad. It's supposed to settle disputes between the miners. Sometimes it works"—he shrugged—"sometimes not. Pa used to be on it. He's one of the original miners, so he knows everybody. Folks like him and trust him." Jem let out a big breath. "That's probably why they hired him to be sheriff."

Unfortunately, he added silently. He glanced down the boardwalk in the direction Pa and No-luck Casey had run.

"How much longer must we stand around?" Aunt Rose asked with a sudden, impatient sigh. "Nathan and I are exhausted. That never-ending stagecoach ride jarred every bone in our bodies." She gave Jem a weak smile. "I believe your father asked you to fetch the wagon, did he not?"

"Yes, ma'am," Jem said. "Sorry. It's been a long day for Ellie and me."

"That's for sure," Ellie agreed.

Jem looked at her. No more school today! Maybe Pa would change his mind about tomorrow too. *He might need my help settling the kinfolk.*

That cheerful thought energized Jem long enough to tell Ellie to keep Aunt Rose and Nathan company while he went after the wagon. Then he clattered down the boardwalk, back the way they'd come earlier that afternoon.

Jem's route out of town took him past the saloon—and the fight. He willed himself not to stop. *Fetch the wagon! Let Pa do his job!* But his good intentions were shattered as a crowd of flailing bodies erupted through the Big Strike's doors and into the street right in front of him.

Jem gasped and froze in place. Dakota no longer had his long knife. It now resided in Frenchy's hand, and the tall, dark miner looked like he knew how to use it. With one quick swipe, the knife slashed across Dakota's arm. He yelped and flinched, clutching his arm. Blood streamed out from between his fingers. The rest of the crowd pushed forward, shouting their encouragement.

Where's Pa? I thought he was going to—

The sudden *crack* of a gunshot and a bellow from Frenchy turned the miners to stone. At Frenchy's feet lay the Arkansas toothpick, shot clean out of his hand. "The next man who even twitches will need Doc Martin's services," Pa said from the doorway of the Big Strike. "I warned you. Now, break it up. We're all going to—"

Jem didn't wait around to hear what his father intended to do next. He'd seen enough. The sight of the unruly miners reveling, and seeing Dakota clutching his blood-soaked sleeve, gave wings to Jem's feet. Without looking back, he took off running for the ranch.

The Coulter spread lay a scant two miles from town. Jem knew he set a record getting there this afternoon. His heart was still racing as he jogged up the dirt lane. He collapsed against the pasture gate and sucked in huge gulps of air to catch his breath.

A few minutes later, Jem swung the gate open and whistled for the horses. A copper-colored gelding gave an answering whinny and trotted over to Jem, shaking his mane. A dapple-gray horse quickly followed.

"Howdy, fellas." Jem rubbed their noses. "We got work to do."

He quickly led Copper and Quicksilver to the wagon and hitched them up. Just as Jem was about to swing up on the wagon seat, a faint barking caught his attention. A large, golden dog came bounding through the fields, yipping his joy at seeing Jem. The dog jumped up and put his paws against the back of the wagon, wagging his tail and whining.

Jem laughed. "All right, Nugget," he said, walking around to the back of the wagon, "you're welcome to come with me to meet the new kinfolk." He worked the brackets loose and lowered the tailgate. Nugget took a flying leap into the wagon bed. He made his way to the high seat, where he took up his post and waited.

Jem closed the tailgate and climbed up on the seat. With a jerk, he released the brake and chirruped to the horses. Nugget barked his eagerness.

The trip back took half the time. The hilly, tree-lined ranch road was not nearly as muddy as the town's streets, and the two horses trotted along tirelessly. Jem slowed the team only when they came to the outskirts of town where the mud got thicker. He didn't *want* to slow down. Jem wanted to urge the horses into a gallop, much like Walt had done bringing in the stagecoach. He liked to see the mud fly from the horses' hooves and hear the harness jingle.

But Jem could not afford more trouble today. If one drop of mud splattered a passerby because of his tomfoolery, Pa would have a conniption fit. He kept the horses to a walk and rounded the corner to the Wells Fargo office.

The stagecoach was gone, no doubt getting cleaned up and readied for the trip out of town in the morning. Jem pulled the wagon into place alongside the boardwalk and looked around. A pile of baggage lay in a jumbled heap, waiting for pickup.

His aunt, cousin, and sister were nowhere in sight.

CHAPTER 6

Miners' Court

Jem let out a long, slow breath. "Hang it all, Nugget. I ran all the way out to the ranch, hitched up the wagon, and raced back to town without resting. I wasn't gone that long. Where'd they go?"

Nugget thumped his tail and swiped his panting tongue across Jem's chin. Jem brushed his dog's sloppy kiss away. Then he jammed the heavy wagon's brake into place and jumped down. Mud squished around his ankles. "Stay in the wagon, boy."

Sometimes Nugget obeyed Jem; sometimes he didn't. Today the dog cocked his head, as if trying to decide if Jem really meant what he said. He whined and gave his tail a sharp slap against the wagon seat.

"Uh-uh." Jem wagged a finger at his friend. "I mean it. You stay here until I get back, or next time I won't bring you along. Ya hear?" He tried to sound like Pa, full of authority. Nugget always obeyed Pa.

Nugget yawned, then jumped down from the seat and into the wagon bed. He turned around once, twice, three times, and collapsed in a heap of golden fur. He laid his head on his paws and gave Jem a mournful look.

42

"Good dog," Jem praised him. "I'll be right back, soon as I find everybody."

Nugget's tail thumped.

Happy that his dog had obeyed him for once, Jem crossed the boardwalk and poked his head into the Express office. "What happened to the two stage passengers who were standing out front with Ellie?" he asked Josh Franklin, the desk clerk.

"Those your kinfolk from back East?" the young man asked. When Jem nodded, he said, "I heard the lady ask your sister if there was any place in this *mud hole*"—he frowned—"where a body could get a bite to eat and wait for the wagon."

Jem winced at Aunt Rose's description of Goldtown— mostly because it was true. Winter and spring were not kind to the town.

"I think they headed down to the Skillet," Josh finished. "It wasn't but a few minutes ago."

With a wave of thanks, Jem turned and hurried down the boardwalk toward the café. If Aunt Rose was buying a late lunch for Nathan and herself, then maybe—just maybe— she'd offer to buy Jem a piece of cornbread, with a bit of molasses dripping over the sides. His mouth watered just thinking about it.

Jem quickened his step. Deep in thought, wondering if Aunt Rose might also buy him a sarsaparilla to wash down the cornbread, he smacked head-on into Will Sterling.

Ooof! Jem stumbled backward.

"Watch where you're going!" Will hollered, brushing off his shirt and trousers. He gave Jem a fierce look. "Can't a fella walk down the street without getting bowled over?"

Jem clamped his jaw shut and resisted the urge to shove weasel-faced Will off the walk and into the mud. He had to clench his fists to do it. That was the only way his hands stayed at his sides. He'd learned the hard way that a fight with Will Sterling never turned out well.

Not that he couldn't lick Will! He could . . . and he had. More than once. But it wasn't worth it. Will was either too dumb or too cocky to remember the lesson. Besides, Jem delivered firewood to the Sterlings. He couldn't afford to lose their business on account of not getting along with Will.

"Where were *you* all afternoon?" Will asked. He straightened his cap over his unruly black curls and folded his arms across his chest. "Miss Cheney went on a rant for a good long time."

"I don't see what business it is of yours where I've been," Jem said, bristling.

"I s'pose not," Will agreed. He looked smugly satisfied. "I had to fetch your pa for Miss Cheney. He was up to his elbows in dirt and mud, trying to talk ol' Nine Toes out of his newest claim."

Jem shrugged. "So what?"

"I didn't know your pa's the new sheriff." He gave Jem a look of sympathy. "I reckon it's tough luck for you."

"How's that?" Jem challenged. He knew Will's sympathy was as phony as fool's gold.

"Well, you gotta live up to being a sheriff's kid now. You know, set a good, law-abiding example for the rest of us sinners. Reckon that means no more playing hooky from school." He shook his head. "I feel kinda sorry for you, Jem. It's about as bad off as being the preacher's kid, if you ask me."

"I'm not asking you," Jem snapped. Will's words hit him hard, mostly because he'd been thinking the very same thing. He didn't like how it sounded coming from Will. He took a step forward. "Get out of my way, Will. I'm in a hurry."

"So am I," Will said. "There's big doin's down at the saloon. Frenchy sliced up Dako—"

"I know," Jem cut him off with a wave and kept walking.

"It's not over," Will went on. "I heard two others got into it and it's a mess. They're holding court right now."

Jem paused. "What about my pa? Is he all right?"

"How do *I* know?" Will said, coming up beside him. "I'm on my way to see—"

Jem took off down the sidewalk, dodging passersby and dogs and peddlers' carts with the ease of much practice. He heard the slapping of boot soles behind him and knew Will was hot on his heels.

Just outside the entrance to the Big Strike, the boys came to a stop. A large crowd overflowed the building, spilling onto the wooden sidewalk. It looked like everybody in town wanted to catch a glimpse of the excitement inside the noisy, ramshackle saloon.

"What do you suppose is happening in there?" Jem asked.

"I dunno," Will replied. "But it's sure drawn a crowd."

Jem jumped up a few times, trying to peek over the men's shoulders, but he couldn't see a thing. Next to him, his friend Cole had found a perch on top of the hitching rail. He stood on tiptoe, gripping a post and peering into the darkened saloon.

"What's going on in there, Cole?" Jem called up to him. *I have to find out if Pa's all right!* His father had broken up the fight, but tempers must have heated up again since then. The new sheriff might still be in the middle of it.

Cole looked down. "I'm not sure. I was walkin' home from school and heard about a fight, and knives, and blood an' all, and how there's gonna be a miners' court. It was already crowded when I got here, so I hiked myself up on the rail." He grinned. "I'll sell you my spot for a nickel. I've seen enough."

"Haven't got a nickel," Jem said. "Leastways, not on me." He did have his precious gold nugget, but he wasn't about to give *that* up.

"Your pa's in there, Jem," Cole went on. "He was in the thick of things for a while. Now he's doing a lot of talking."

"Is he all right?" Jem held his breath for the answer.

"I think so, but"—Cole frowned—"he's got a lot of blood smeared on him."

Right then, Jem forgot about his errand, the wagon, his kinfolk, and even the possibility of cornbread and molasses. He tried to squeeze through the crowd of burly men choking the doorway. It was like trying to shove his way through a brick wall.

A huge, hairy arm ended Jem's effort to wiggle his way into the saloon. "Get back, boy," a deep voice growled. "Ain't no room in there. You'll get trampled."

Jem backed away. "I gotta see what's going on!"

"I'll give you a nickel, Cole," Will said. "The miners' court is always interesting to watch, and—"

"Oh, no, you won't!" Jem broke in. He looked up at his friend. "How would you like to add the Big Strike to your sawdust customers? It's worth a heap more'n Will's measly nickel."

Cole gaped at Jem. "Are you funnin' me? You'd trade the best sawdust customer in town for this spot?" He shook his head. "What's the catch?"

"No catch. Cross my heart. It's yours." *Since Pa won't let me keep it anyway,* he added silently.

"It's a trade." Cole jumped down, and the boys shook hands. "The rail and post are all yours."

Before Will could beat him to it, Jem climbed up the hitching rail and steadied himself against the post. Then he leaned as far forward as he could to get a good look.

There wasn't much to see inside the darkened, smoky saloon. Jem was glad he hadn't traded away anything of real value for this spot. When his eyes adjusted to the gloom inside, he could make out the long, rough-hewn boards that served as the bar. Behind the bar, Mr. Tobias, the saloon's owner, stood with a grim look on his face and a shotgun cradled in his arms.

Looks like he's trying to keep his place from getting torn apart again, Jem thought. The Big Strike saw its share of fights and rowdy behavior, especially on Saturday nights, after the miners' payday. Mr. Tobias was always making repairs to his tables, chairs, and shelves.

An insistent tug on Jem's trouser leg yanked him around.

"What's goin' on?" Will asked.

"I didn't trade with Cole so I could be the town crier. Let me be." Jem shook off Will's grip and went back to watching.

It looked like Cole and Will were right about holding a miners' court. The mayor and the town council had set it up right then and there. No warning, no courthouse, no judge; and no jury today either, except for the crowd.

Jem wondered how they would vote, and who would get whipped or run out of town this time. "Wish I could vote," he muttered. "I'd vote to run 'em all out." He was tired of Pa being yanked into the rowdy miners' troubles, sheriff or not.

"What did you say?" Will demanded in his usual whine. "C'mon, Jem. Tell me. I'll . . . I'll give you the nickel I offered Cole if you just tell me what's going on."

A nickel is a nickel, Jem decided.

He watched and listened for a few minutes, then said, "It looks like it's about over, but there's still a lot of hollering going on. They say Frenchy wrestled the knife from Dakota, with the help of a couple of new miners who've been hanging around lately." He paused for breath. "Dakota's arm is wrapped up, but it's not doing much good. Lots of blood's still seeping through. They say he'd be dead if the sheriff hadn't stepped in. So it's"—Jem strained to hear the rest— "attempted murder." He shuddered. "Dakota's not saying much. He looks kinda pale, like all the fight's gone out of him."

Jem glanced around the darkened building, searching for his father. Pa stood against the bar, arms folded over his chest, watching the noisy proceedings. Jem sighed his relief. Pa didn't look injured, or even worried. Sure, his shirt and vest were smeared dark with what must be blood, but it was probably Dakota's blood. *He's all right!*

Across the room, three dirty, unshaven miners glowered at the new sheriff. Blood splattered their faces, and two of the men wore rough slings on their arms. Frenchy stood with them, breathing heavily, as if he were getting ready to challenge the court's decision. He appeared uninjured, except for a bandaged hand.

When the vote came, Pa lifted his hand and quickly returned it to his chest. Dozens of other hands went up, then down, and Mayor Gordon whacked his fist against the bar. A cheer rose.

"The miners' court just voted to throw Frenchy and those others out of town," Jem reported to Will. "I guess he tried to jump Dakota's claim once too often. The attempted murder charge didn't help him much either. Frenchy looks madder than a peeled rattler."

"That's it? It's over?" Will pouted. "That ain't worth a nickel."

Jem didn't reply. Worth it or not, Will owed him a nickel, and he'd better pay.

The crowd began to break up. Men from inside pushed their way through the crush of bodies and out into the late afternoon sun.

Jem took one last look. "A bunch of men are guarding Frenchy and the others. Looks like they're getting ready to show 'em the road out of town. The mayor and town council are standing around my pa, talking to him and Dakota. Your pa's there too."

"My father's in there?" Will asked. He looked worried. "I didn't know he was back in town. What's he saying?"

"I can't hear. It's too noisy," Jem replied. He jumped down

from the hitching rail and held out his hand. "The crowd's thinning out. Give me the nickel and you can go in and see for yourself."

Will dropped a nickel into Jem's open palm. "Nah, I've heard enough. I think I'll head home before—"

"Before your pa catches you here, right?" Jem grinned, pocketing the money. "For once, Will, I agree with you. I better find Ellie and my new kinfolk. I'm supposed to take 'em back to the ranch and settle everybody in."

Will looked full of questions, but he didn't ask any. Jem was glad. Goldtown would learn about Aunt Rose and Nathan soon enough. Without saying good-bye, the mine owner's son scurried away and disappeared into the crowd.

Jem turned to go and nearly smacked into a giant figure wearing a long, black overcoat. He stumbled back in surprise at the sight of Frenchy staring down at him from under dark, bushy eyebrows.

"S-sorry, Mr. DuBois," Jem stammered. Nobody called the miner "Frenchy" to his face.

Frenchy grunted. Then slowly, he leaned toward Jem. "This was once a fine gold camp, boy. People minded their own business. But no longer. Not with the preachers going after the miners and trying to save their souls. And now"— his bushy brows came together—"we must put up with a sheriff besides." He turned and spat. "Your *père* better be careful, or he will be the first and *last* sheriff of Goldtown."

"Shut up, DuBois," a miner growled. "Keep moving." He shoved Frenchy along the boardwalk, toward the outskirts of town. His comrades trailed behind, each accompanied by an armed man.

Jem watched the guilty miners being escorted out of Goldtown. He couldn't help trembling, and his stomach churned. He didn't know if it was from Frenchy's words or from hunger. Jem sighed. It was unlikely Aunt Rose and Ellie were still waiting for him at the café. Too bad. Cornbread would have tasted mighty good.

"If I know Ellie," he mused aloud, "she got tired of waiting and took Aunt Rose back to the Express office. She probably asked Mr. Franklin to load the baggage and then drove everybody out to the ranch herself."

"She better not have," Pa said from the saloon's doorway, "seeing as I asked *you* to do it."

Jem whirled. And groaned.

⤙ CHAPTER 7 ⤚

Everything's Upside Down

Matt Coulter covered the distance between Jem and himself in two long strides. "Why aren't you doing what I asked? By now you should be home, with your aunt and cousin resting on the porch. Instead, you're hanging around the saloon."

"Aunt Rose wasn't there when I . . . and I . . . I was worried about you, Pa," Jem tried to explain. "I heard there was a miners' court, and . . ." He hung his head.

"Never mind." Pa grasped Jem's arm and hurried him down the boardwalk at a dead run. He didn't waste breath on an extended scolding. Jem didn't need one. He knew he was in trouble. The wagon was heavy, and Ellie was too little to drive it.

"I'm sure she didn't really try to drive the wagon," Jem panted, running to keep up with his father's long strides. "Ellie knows better." *Please, God,* he prayed, *surely You gave her more sense than that!*

Pa didn't answer.

Jem's heart sank to his boots when he and his father pounded to a stop in front of the Wells Fargo office. The baggage was gone, the wagon was gone, and the office clerk was standing out in front.

"You just missed 'em," Josh said. "I loaded up the baggage, but before I could turn around, that girl of yours slapped the reins and took off down the street. I hollered at her to stop, but she just kept going." He paused. "I'm sorry, Matt. I thought for sure she'd wait for you or Jem."

"Not your fault," Pa said. He released Jem's arm and hastened for the hitching rail across the street. "You're gonna walk home, boy," he called over his shoulder to Jem. "Take your time. Think about all the poor choices you made today." Then he untied the reins of his large black gelding, swung into the saddle, and galloped toward the ranch.

Josh gave a low whistle. "Sounds like you're in a heap of trouble, Jem." He shook his head and ducked back into the office.

Jem watched his father race his horse through town, mud splattering every which way. King could easily carry two riders, but today he was carrying only one. "I wish I hadn't run into Will," Jem mumbled. He wanted to kick himself. "I should've gone straight to the café."

Jem clomped down the boardwalk past the Big Strike saloon. The place was quiet now, and he remembered he had to trudge back later with his bags of sawdust. It made him tired just thinking about it. He turned the corner that would take him out of town and back to the ranch. Oaks, a few pines, and some cottonwood shaded parts of the road as it meandered between the low-lying hills.

Jem took his time. Hopefully, Pa would overtake the wagon right away, tie up King, and drive everybody home. He'd give Ellie a piece of his mind for thinking she was big enough to drive the wagon. And by the time Jem got back to the ranch, the crisis would be over and Pa would have simmered down. He slowed his pace to a crawl.

Twenty minutes later and only halfway home, Jem reached down and snatched up a rock from the dirt road. Taking aim, he hurled it at a knothole in the trunk of a giant oak. *Plunk!*

The rock bounced off the tree and fell to the ground. Jem threw another rock, then another. Each stone hit the mark dead-center. Nobody could pitch a rock—or a ball—as far or as fast or as accurately as Jeremiah Coulter. He was always chosen first for a game of stickball.

Right now, Jem wished he'd stayed at school and played stickball during noon recess rather than taking off for his gold-panning venture. He fingered the gold in his pocket and sighed, long and deep. He wouldn't be seeing any more nuggets for quite some time—not with over a month of school left.

The sound of galloping hooves a few minutes later brought Jem's head up from searching the ground for another stone to throw. His sister was astride Copper, wisps of her auburn hair whipping around her face. It matched the horse's coloring exactly.

"Jem!" Ellie shouted, bringing Copper to a sudden stand-still. The horse sidestepped and tossed his head.

Jem reached out his free hand and took hold of the bridle. "Easy, fella." He looked at Ellie. "Where are you headed?"

"I came to find you." She slid off the horse and handed the reins to her brother. "What's taking you so long to get home?"

Jem shrugged. "I'm giving Pa time to cool off." Then he burst out, "What were you *thinking*, Ellie? You're too little to drive the wagon. Why didn't you wait for me?" He grabbed a fistful of Copper's mane and swung himself up on the horse's bare back. Then he glared down at his sister, whose eyes had widened at his words.

"I'm sorry I got you in trouble," Ellie said. "It doesn't seem fair that you have to walk home on account of me, so I came to give you a ride."

Jem's anger dissolved at Ellie's apology. "Does Pa know you're here?" If Ellie had sneaked off to help him . . .

She nodded. "I don't think he's sore at you anymore,

Jem, once he saw we were all right." She ducked her head. "I pulled the wagon over just outside town. Aunt Rose was pitching a fit about me driving the horses; Nathan kept trying to take over; and Nugget was barking. There was enough noise to wake snakes. I decided I better wait for you or Pa."

So, she's got some sense after all, Jem thought in relief.

Ellie looked up. "Pa looked mighty glad to see us. He hugged me and only scolded me a little. Then he drove us back to the ranch. I asked if I could fetch you home on Copper and he said yes."

Jem grinned and held out his hand. "Come on. Mount up."

Ellie took Jem's hand and scrambled up behind him. She settled herself on Copper's rump and grasped Jem's suspenders to keep her balance as he urged the horse into a lope. They would be home in no time now.

"Slow down!" Ellie yelled in his ear. "I'm not in any hurry to get home. That's the other reason I wanted to find you, Jem. I gotta talk to you."

Jem slowed Copper to a plodding walk. A minute went by, then two. He frowned. "I thought you wanted to talk." When she didn't answer, he turned around and looked at her impatiently. "What's the matter?"

"Nothin'." Ellie sniffed.

Jem knew better. His sister was never shy with words. "Nothin'" meant something was dreadfully wrong.

"Listen, Ellie," he said, bringing Copper to a standstill. "We're almost home. If you've got somethin' to say, then you better come right out and say it."

"It . . . it's too mean to say, but I gotta tell somebody, and not Pa. It would hurt his feelings."

Jem stared straight ahead and waited. Copper stood still, swishing his tail at the annoying flies buzzing around the travelers. The only sounds came from Ellie's sniffing and a chattering squirrel in a nearby oak tree.

Finally, she spoke. "Everything's all wrong, Jem. Upside-down wrong. Aunt Rose and Nathan are moving in. And . . . and I don't want them to!"

Jem frowned. "Is that all? Of course they're moving in. I don't want them here either, but kinfolk take care of each other. It's not like it's a surprise or anything. We read the letter last fall, remember?"

"But I didn't think they'd change things. You didn't hear Aunt Rose and Pa talking about it on the way home. They're changing *everything*."

"How can they?" Jem asked. Their small place was more like a cabin than a real house. Three rooms downstairs. An attic loft, where he and Ellie slept and kept their things, separated by an old blanket that hung from a rope strung across the ceiling. A privy out back. A woodshed. A henhouse. A rickety old barn. How could anybody—even a city aunt—change *that*?

Ellie clamped her fingers around Jem's suspenders, as if she were ready for a sudden burst of speed from Copper. "Pa's giving Aunt Rose his room downstairs," she said. "And Nathan is sleeping up in the attic with you. In my half. Aunt Rose says I can't sleep up there anymore, and Pa agreed. The attic is for you *boys*." She sounded angry. Jem didn't blame her.

"But where will *you* sleep?" he asked. A little itch in the back of his mind needed scratching. Nathan upstairs, invading his and Ellie's attic space? Their aunt in Pa's room? Maybe Ellie was right. Maybe Pa and Aunt Rose could change everything, after all.

Ellie dug her heels into Copper's flank, and the horse bounded forward.

"Whoa, there!" Jem pulled back on the reins. "Stop it, Ellie."

"But I'm so *mad*," she confessed. "I have to sleep with Aunt Rose, in Pa's room. In the same bed even, since it's big

enough. Aunt Rose says relatives sleep in the same bed all
the time. I never heard of that, but Pa said the same thing."

The itch inside Jem's head got itchier. If Aunt Rose and
Ellie slept in Pa's room . . .

"Where's Pa going to sleep?" he asked.

Ellie shrugged. "I don't know. Maybe on the floor or out
in the barn, until he can build another room."

Jem didn't like this idea one bit. Things were upside
down for sure! "Maybe I'll sleep out in the barn with Pa," he
muttered. "It would be a heap better than staying in the attic
with our cousin."

"Me too," Ellie said with a sudden lilt in her voice. "That's
a jim-dandy idea!"

Jem groaned. That would shame Pa even more, not to
mention insult their guests.

"Ellie," he said, "I was just thinking out loud. I'm not
really going to sleep in the barn, and neither are you. We've
got bigger trouble than where we're going to sleep." He
twisted around and gave Ellie a serious look. "Did you see
what Pa was wearing today?"

She closed her eyes and crinkled her eyebrows, which was
Ellie's way of remembering. "Same as always," she answered.
"Denim britches, gray shirt, black hat, boots—"

"Roasted rattlesnakes, Ellie! Not his clothes! That . . . that
. . . *sheriff's* badge. That shiny, silver star that makes him a
target same as if he was wearing a sign that says 'Shoot me.'"

Ellie sucked in her breath. "I don't want Pa to be sheriff."

"Me neither," Jem said. "It was all right, I reckon, when
Pa helped out and was on the miners' court. He was being a
good neighbor and could say no if he wanted to." Jem shook
his head. "But now Pa will *have* to go after outlaws, on account
of it's his job. And . . . outlaws don't like sheriffs."

Jem had a lot more he wanted to say, but a sliver of good
sense kept his mouth shut. It would be best not to scare Ellie.

He nudged Copper into a fast walk and kept his thoughts to himself.

Worrying about his father chasing down outlaws or officially breaking up lawlessness in Goldtown was only one of Jem's troubles. Being a sheriff's kid would also be hard to live with. *Everybody always watching to make sure I set a good example. Folks always ready to remind me when I'm not.*

Jem had no wish to run wild like the no-account rowdies who broke windows, beat up other kids, and snitched candy from the mercantile. Boys like that gave the Ladies' Missionary Society plenty of opportunities to pray for their souls and try to set them on the right path.

But Jem did not want to be under a magnifying glass either, always worrying about living up to the standards of being the sheriff's boy.

"Wonder what the other kids'll say when they find out," Ellie murmured.

Jem winced. Will Sterling had already given him a taste of that. Leave it to Ellie to say out loud what he was thinking.

There was no more time for talk. Copper trotted through the wide-open, broken ranch gate and up the short drive to the yard. Noisy yapping greeted Jem and Ellie. Nugget was barking and leaping at something in one of the tall oak trees that grew like weeds all over the ranch.

"Looks like Nugget's treed a varmint," Ellie said, chuckling. "Run get the shotgun, Jem. Maybe it's a raccoon. Didn't you want a cap made from—"

"It's no 'coon, Ellie," Jem said, sliding off Copper's back. "Not in the middle of the afternoon." He pointed. "It's not a four-legged varmint at all."

⇥ CHAPTER 8 ⇤

City Cousin

"**C**ousin!" Nathan's shout came loud and desperate. "Call off your dog. He chased me up this ol' tree and won't let me down. I've been calling for Uncle Matthew, but nobody can hear me over this yapping beast."

Jem gave a short, sharp whistle. "Here, Nugget. Come here, fella."

Tail wagging, the golden dog barked one last time at the boy in the tree, then bounded across the yard to greet Jem and Ellie. Together, they headed back to the oak. Six or seven rough, narrow slats had been nailed up the trunk to allow for handholds. Twelve feet above ground, a rectangular platform squeezed between the spreading branches.

Nathan lay on his belly, peering over the edge of the uneven planks.

Jem pressed his lips together to keep from smiling. Laughter gushed up, but he choked it back and jabbed an elbow into Ellie, who was giggling.

"Shhh," he hissed. Then he called out to the figure above, "You can come down now. I don't know what got into that dog. He usually only chases cats and 'coons and squirrels up trees." Jem scratched his head. "And you don't look like any of those."

"Maybe he smells like one," Ellie whispered, which earned her another sharp poke in the ribs.

Slowly, Nathan turned around and scooted over the edge of the platform, feet first. For an instant he hung suspended, until one booted toe found the makeshift ladder rung. He began to cautiously make his way down.

Just then the lowest slat snapped. Nathan lost his footing and landed on the ground with a hard *thud*. He yelped.

Nugget bounded forward, but Jem grabbed a handful of fur just in time and yanked the dog back. "Stay!" he ordered. Nugget sat down and whined, but he remained at Jem's side.

"Are you all right?" Ellie squeaked.

Groaning, Nathan pushed himself up from the ground. He didn't say a word while he brushed the dirt, twigs, and dead leaves from his backside. The mud from town had dried in splotches all over his knickers and jacket. His cap was missing, and his hands were scratched and bleeding. The scratches matched a scrape on his cheek. Nathan looked miserable and out of place standing under a tree in the middle of the California foothills.

Jem felt a twinge of sympathy—not much, but just enough to let his imagination carry him to the center of Boston, Massachusetts. He saw himself standing in the middle of a busy cobblestone street, gawking at the tall buildings and trolley cars, and not knowing what to say. Or where to go. Or how to act. Worse, there would be plenty of city folks ready to make fun of him for how he talked or dressed.

I'd feel just as out of place back East as Nathan is probably feeling right now, Jem thought.

He thrust out his hand. "Welcome to the Coulter ranch, Nathan. It's not much, but we haven't starved yet. Sorry about Nugget. I don't know why Pa didn't come out and make him mind. Probably thought he was chasing a squirrel. He's a good watch dog though. If he sees us shaking hands, he'll know you're a friend."

Nathan gave Nugget a wary glance, then clasped Jem's hand. Some of his tension seemed to melt away, but he didn't smile.

Jem laughed and clapped Nathan on the shoulder. "Sure wish I could've seen you scoot up that tree. By the look of your hands and face, I bet you set a record."

The ghost of a smile appeared on Nathan's face. He turned his hands over and studied the scratches. "I didn't even notice. I just wanted to get away from that dog. He was eyeing me real mean back in the wagon. I knew he was sizing me up and deciding he didn't like me."

Jem lost his grin. *Another reason I shouldn't have stopped by the saloon.* Nugget did not like strangers. He was a one-family dog. Pa had probably been too busy driving the wagon and talking to Aunt Rose to introduce Nugget to the newest members of the family.

Jem would not have forgotten. And Nathan wouldn't have had to scramble up a tree. "I'm sorry," he said. "This has not turned out to be one of my best days."

"Mine either," Ellie said.

Nathan gave his cousins a questioning look.

"Pa caught Ellie and me playing hooky this afternoon," Jem explained. "We were panning for gold out at the creek. It was the first nice day this spring, and I couldn't stay in that classroom one minute longer."

To Jem's surprise, Nathan nodded. "I don't blame you. Last year, a bunch of us snuck down to the docks to watch a whaling ship come in." He winced. "The schoolmaster blistered our backsides when he found out. Father was off fighting in the War, or I'd have gotten it from him too."

Jem's interest rose a notch. *My tenderfoot, slicked-up, city-*

raised cousin, playing hooky? Bully for him! Maybe there was more to Nathan than he'd seen so far.

"We've been in trouble ever since Pa caught us, and the day's not over yet," Jem said. "I've gotta go back to town and deliver eight bags of sawdust to the saloon. Then, I've got to chop firewood for a couple of my customers. But I can't do any of that until I finish my chores around here first." He let out a frustrated breath.

Then a new thought hit Jem like a flash. He peered at his cousin. "How old are you?"

"Huh? I'm eleven. What of it?"

"That's plenty old," Jem said. His grin returned.

"Plenty old for what?" Ellie and Nathan asked at exactly the same time.

Ellie eyed Jem carefully. "I'm plenty old too," she reminded him. "You're not gonna leave me out of anything."

"I wouldn't leave you out, Ellie. I was just thinking that Nathan's old enough to help us with all the chores around here."

Ellie laughed and clapped her hands. Jem could see her quick brain adding up what an extra pair of hands— two extra pairs if they counted Aunt Rose—would mean. If Nathan was a fast, hard worker, they might get their chores done in half the time, and then . . .

"We'll have more time to work the claim this summer!" Ellie finished Jem's thoughts out loud. She ran to Copper and threw her arms around his neck. Then she led the horse to where Jem and Nathan were still standing under the tree house. "C'mon, Jem. Let's start teaching Nathan right away."

Nathan looked aghast. "Chores? What are you talking about?" He glanced around the unkempt yard and shuddered. "No amount of chores can fix this place up."

Jem's anger spurted, but he choked it back. For the first time, he looked at the ranch with fresh eyes. The tall spring grass was already turning golden. A faded red barn with doors barely hanging on to their rusty hinges rested in a grove of scrub oak. Piles of wood—some cut and stacked, but most scattered in heaps—lay off to one side near a wood-shed. A few split-rail corrals, a beat-up wagon, and a couple of outbuildings in disrepair spread out before him.

No wonder his cousin shuddered. The Coulter ranch was not a pretty picture. But Nathan had no right to spout off about it. Didn't they teach kids manners back East?

"Running a ranch is a *lot* of work," Jem said, narrowing his eyes. "Pa does the best he knows how."

Nathan turned red. "Hey, I'm sorry. I didn't mean to—"

"And we *all* help," Ellie interrupted. "There's milking the cow. Gathering eggs. Chopping wood. Mucking out the barn. Feeding the stock. Mending fences. Rubbing down the horses."

Nathan's eyes grew bigger and more horrified as Ellie ticked off the ranch chores on her fingers.

"And those are just the outside chores," Jem added. "There's inside chores too, but I'm hoping your ma takes over some of those."

"So, Nathan," Ellie said, "Where do you want to start?"
Nathan shook his head and backed away. With a *thunk*, he
fell against the tree trunk. "I c-can't do any of those things."
Jem exchanged a glance with Ellie, then took a step forward. "Can't? Or *won't*? Didn't you do chores back in Boston?"
Nathan looked at his shoes. "We had"—he swallowed—
"servants. Mother expected me to keep my room clean and
pick up after myself, and study hard at school."
Ellie gasped. "You must've been *rich*! Only rich folks have
hired help. Like Will and Maybelle Sterling. They have a
cook and a maid and even a—"
"Oh, Ellie, hush!" Jem interrupted, seeing the stricken
look on Nathan's face. "Sometimes you talk too much. Go
put Copper away."
Ellie clamped her jaw shut. For an instant, it looked like
she might refuse to put up the horse. Then with a huff, she
yanked on Copper's reins and headed for the gate to the
nearby field.
When Jem turned around, Nathan was looking at him.
"Nah, we weren't rich," he said. "Not like real rich folks. But
Father was a captain in the army, so we were better off than
most. And he was gone a lot even before the War broke out."
He paused and took a deep breath. "Mother told me it would
be very different here, but until today I had no idea what that
really meant."
Nathan clenched his fists and stepped away from the
tree. "Listen, Jem. I'm no sissy, no matter what you and your
sister think. Sure, the dog startled me, but I can't go back to
Boston. I have to make the best of it out here." He hesitated,
then burst out, "But I don't know how. Will you . . . will you
help me?" Nathan held Jem's gaze, as if daring his cousin to
tease him for admitting such a weakness.
Jem thought long and hard. Nathan was probably dumber
than a fence post about ranch chores, but he hadn't had a

father around for a long time to teach him anything, the way Pa had taught Ellie and Jem. Besides, Nathan's mother was Pa's sister. That made Nathan partly a Coulter. With God's help, there wasn't anything a Coulter could not tackle and succeed in doing.

Yet, Jem couldn't help scratching at that little itch in the back of his mind. Even if Nathan *was* a Coulter, he was from the city, and a greenhorn besides. Jem had seen his share of greenhorns. Most of them were only worth as much as fool's gold in a pan of gravel. Jem wondered if Nathan would shatter like fool's gold or if he could be molded and proved to be the real thing.

Jem would like a cousin—or any friend—like that.

"I'll help you, Nathan," he said at last, just as Ellie joined them under the tree. "So will Ellie. That's what kinfolk are for. But"—he let out a long, slow breath—"it's not going to be easy. You've got a lot to learn, and . . ."

"You're not going to like it," Ellie finished.

⊰ CHAPTER 9 ⊱

Never-Ending Chores

Just as Jem predicted, Nathan didn't like learning how to do the never-ending chores on the struggling Coulter ranch. Worse, Jem discovered that his cousin didn't like *any-thing* about Goldtown, the ranch, or the surrounding area. He didn't like Nugget, and he was afraid of the milk cow's sharp horns. Even the chickens seemed to have a grudge against him.

"Whack him!" Ellie's shrill command made Jem pause. He looked up from milking and peered through the open barn doors. Just beyond the opening, he saw Nathan flash by.

What's going on now? Jem wondered.

Instead of their cousin helping cut their chore time in half, it took even longer to get things done. During the past month, the pile of wood that needed splitting had grown instead of shrunk, they were often late for school, and Jem's frog and firewood business had slowed to a standstill. By the time he and Ellie helped Nathan learn a new chore, there was no time for anything else.

"Maybe when the school term is over," he told the cow. She mooed and stamped an impatient hoof. Jem milked faster. Good thing he could milk and think at the same time.

Mr. Sims at the café was fit to be tied about the lack of frog legs for his menu. Sadly, since Sundays were rest days, Jem couldn't use those long afternoons to fill his pail with the hoppers. He couldn't even split one log.

"If you can't get it done in six days," Pa was fond of saying, "then I reckon it's not that important. We work hard enough all week. Let's go fishing after church instead."

Well, fishing was fine, and trout were tasty—especially the way Aunt Rose fried them up, but Jem wished he could be making money or at least panning for gold in Cripple Creek. Unfortunately, Pa thought prospecting was work too, and definitely not the proper way to spend a Sunday afternoon. Besides, Jem's panning days were on hold until school was out.

Ellie's shout came again, louder this time. "Kick him, Nathan! Oh, no. *Run!*"

Jem abandoned the milk stool, grabbed the half-full pail of milk, and rushed out of the barn in time to see the door to the chicken house slam shut—with Nathan inside. A large, reddish-brown rooster ran back and forth in front of the old shed. Deep, threatening noises erupted from his throat. Every few seconds, he attacked the shed with his sharp talons, then started his frenzied running all over again.

From Ellie's side, Nugget was barking, which added to the racket.

"Hang it all, Ellie!" Jem yelled. "Can't you teach Nathan to gather eggs without turning it into an all-day chore?"

"I'm tryin'," Ellie shot back. "But Mordecai's taken an awful dislike to him. He goes after him every chance he gets." Armed with a three-foot-long branch, she ran to the rooster and swung the stick across his tail feathers. "Get going!" she shouted. "Shoo!"

Mordecai squawked but held his ground, glaring at Ellie with baleful eyes. He scratched the dirt, ruffled his feathers, and made an attempt to launch himself at her. Just then, a rock whizzed past Ellie and landed between Mordecai's feet. The startled rooster jumped a foot, then retreated around the corner of the shed, cackling his fury all the way.

"You gotta teach me how to do that sometime," Ellie said.

Jem grinned. "It's just a matter of careful aiming, then letting the rock fly." He turned toward the henhouse and called, "You can come out now, Nathan. Make sure you've got those eggs."

Looking sheepish, Nathan exited the shed, carrying a wicker basket. It was heaped full of brown eggs. None looked broken—this time. He scurried past his cousins without a word and ducked through the door of the cabin's lean-to.

Jem and Ellie looked at each other. Jem shrugged. "He's trying his best, I reckon. It's just gonna take a lot longer than we thought. But he'll come around."

"He'd better," Ellie said with a scowl. She patted Nugget, who swished his tail. "Good dog."

Jem handed Ellie the milk pail. "Finish milking for me, will ya? I've still got to bring in the wood." He turned and hurried off to the woodpile.

When the family sat down for breakfast half an hour later, Aunt Rose told the children to bow their heads for the blessing.

"Aren't we gonna wait for Pa?" Ellie asked.

It was strange having a grown-up woman bustling around the stove, cooking up meals that actually tasted good, rather than the concoctions Pa used to throw together. Yet, eating without their father didn't seem right, no matter how hungry Jem might be. He eyed the steaming flapjacks and waited for Aunt Rose's answer.

"He's not here," she said matter-of-factly, picking up her napkin. She spread it over her lap and said a quick prayer. Then she picked up her fork and began to eat.

Nathan dug into his breakfast, but Jem and Ellie stared at their aunt.

"Where is he?" Jem asked. "Out with the cattle? I can send Nugget after him. That way Pa can eat breakfast while it's hot."

Aunt Rose shook her head. "He got called away during the night on sheriff business. There's no telling how long he might be gone this time. I'll keep some pancakes warm for him."

Jem's appetite disappeared. "Pa taking that sheriff's job was a bad idea all the way around," he muttered.

"Jeremiah Isaiah Coulter!"

Jem winced. His aunt sure seemed to like the sound of his full name. She used it plenty, especially when she was firing herself up to give a scolding.

"Being sheriff is a respectable position," Aunt Rose said, eyes flashing. "And that silver star he wears is a badge of honor. Land sakes, child! I'm astonished this town has only now realized they need a sheriff to keep law and order. I'm proud they asked my brother to take the position. You should be proud too." Then she smiled. "The forty dollars they're paying him every month is surely a blessing."

"Goldtown got along fine without a sheriff for years and years," Jem argued. "And we've gotten along fine without the extra cash. I don't know why they had to hire a sheriff now, or why it had to be Pa."

Jem knew he was on shaky ground. His arguing sounded mighty close to backtalk, something Pa never allowed. "I'm sorry, Aunt Rose," he apologized quickly. "I don't mean to contradict, but you don't know Goldtown. Killings and claim jumpings and drunks are just a small part of what goes on in town. It's dangerous being a sheriff."

"But necessary," Aunt Rose insisted. Her voice softened. "It's only a part-time job, Jeremiah, and you have to admit we need the money. God will protect Matthew. He'll be fine. Don't carry on so."

Easier said than done. Jem picked at his breakfast and couldn't help but notice that Ellie was doing the same. Only Nathan seemed unaffected. He gobbled up six molasses-drenched flapjacks and chugged down a tall glass of milk in no time. *Our cousin sure knows how to pack away the food,* Jem thought.

Since Aunt Rose had taken over the cooking, Jem found himself eating more too. Instead of a hunk of bread or a stale biscuit and a wizened apple for his noon meal, he often had a real sandwich, thick with fresh butter. Sometimes a rare molasses cookie was slipped inside his lunch pail as a surprise.

Jem was almost ready to give in and admit that having Aunt Rose take over the household was not a bad thing. If only she would content herself with just managing the house and stop trying to manage his and Ellie's lives! She expected Jem to run a comb through his hair every day and wear a clean shirt. Ellie had to sit still and learn to sew samplers in the evenings. Worse, Aunt Rose wanted to know where they were every minute. That was hard to swallow. Just because so many things out here frightened her, it was no reason to keep everybody on a short leash.

Good thing Pa agreed and set her straight, Jem thought, *or we'd be stuck on the ranch all summer.* He asked to be excused and pushed back from the table. "I'll get Copper ready to take us to school."

"I'm sorry, Jeremiah," Aunt Rose said. "Matthew told me he needs the horses later today when he returns. You children will have to walk to school."

Jem stared mutely at Aunt Rose as her words sank in. Then he yanked Ellie up from her chair. "We've got to leave right now, or we'll be late again." He was mighty tired of copying lines about punctuality. "C'mon, Ellie. Nathan. We gotta fly!"

Without another word, Jem snatched up his lunch pail and hurried across the room. He didn't look back when Aunt Rose insisted Ellie's hair needed brushing. Ellie didn't look back either. They were out the door and down the drive in less than a minute, with Nathan only a few steps behind.

"We won't be late today," Jem vowed, "even if we have to run all the way!"

⊰ CHAPTER 10 ⊱

Back to the Creek

Thankfully, the term ended the following week. After enduring an evening at the school exhibition for parents and the school board, Jem was finally free from his brick prison. He celebrated by rolling out of bed at the crack of dawn the next day and dragging Nathan with him. His cousin groaned but followed Jem sleepily down the ladder and outside to get a head start on the day's chores.

"What is the all-fired hurry, Cousin? There's no school to rush off to." Nathan yawned and swung the axe over his head. Down it came with a solid *whack* into the stump, missing the log he intended to split. Jem patiently set it upright again.

"Once our chores are done, we get the day to ourselves," Jem replied. "I have frogs to catch for Mr. Sims and firewood to cut and deliver to three customers, but that can wait one more day." He smiled broadly. "To celebrate my first day out of school, I'm heading out to our claim as quick as I can. Pa said I couldn't pan gold 'til the term ended. Well, it ended yesterday and I'm going out there today. Strike probably wonders where I've been."

Whack! The log cracked down the middle, and the two halves tumbled to the ground. "Who's Strike?" Nathan asked.

Jem took the axe from Nathan and split three logs before answering. "Strike-it-rich Sam is an old prospector, a friend, and my partner. Our gold claim is right next to his, out on Cripple Creek." He split three more logs. "You'll meet him soon enough . . . that is, if you want to come panning for gold with Ellie and me."

"I do!" Nathan said. His eyes gleamed with a look Jem knew well.

Just like every other greenhorn who thinks gold is lying around for the taking, Jem noted. *Maybe it was lying around back in '49, but it's sure not anymore.* The faint, faraway banging of the stamp mill reminded Jem how rare placer gold was these days.

He handed the axe back to Nathan. "All right, then. See how fast you can get the wood split. A dozen more should be enough for today. Do you think you can get it done before I finish the milking?"

Nathan looked from the pile of logs to the small stack of split wood. Then he gripped the axe and nodded. "Possibly. As long as you milk real slow."

Jem did not milk "real slow." He flew through his chores, then finished splitting the last few logs for Nathan. Both boys hauled the wood inside to the woodbox, so Aunt Rose would have plenty of fuel to feed the large, black cook stove. The coffee pot was boiling and bacon sizzling when the boys slammed through the back door with the final load.

Pa sat at the kitchen table, sipping coffee and reading a week-old copy of the *San Francisco Bulletin*. He put down the newspaper when the boys joined him. "You two are up mighty early this morning."

"Yes, sir," Jem said. "I'm taking Nathan out to the claim as soon as our chores are done. Hopefully before midday." He paused. "I mean, if it's all right with you and Aunt Rose."

Aunt Rose paused in her bacon-frying and wrinkled her forehead in thought. "I suppose I can get along without you for a few hours today," she finally agreed. "So long as you don't make a habit of it all summer."

Jem let out the breath he'd been holding.

"It's fine with me," Pa said, smiling. He downed his coffee with one last gulp and swept the paper aside. "Between the ranch and town, I've got myself a full day, so you make sure Rose doesn't need you to fetch and carry for her before you disappear. The garden might need your attention too."

Jem groaned. Before Aunt Rose's arrival, the Coulter ranch did not boast any kind of vegetable garden. Pa had too much else to do, and Jem and Ellie knew nothing about tending a patch of weedy ground.

Aunt Rose changed all that not long after she moved in. It had taken her no time at all to talk her brother into plowing up a large kitchen garden in a sunny patch of ground. It was true Jem liked eating what Aunt Rose grew, but he hated weeding and hauling water.

"Yes, Pa," he said, hoping it would stay cool enough today to keep the garden from getting too thirsty.

Jem nodded his thanks when Aunt Rose plunked a steaming platter of bacon and eggs in front of him. Then she did the same for Nathan. Ellie slammed through the back door, carefully set the basket of eggs on the counter, and plopped down next to her brother. As soon as Pa said the blessing, Jem dug into his breakfast.

"I won't be home for supper tonight, Rosie," Pa said, reaching for the pepper. "I'll work around here this morning, but I'll be tied up in town the rest of the day. Sheriff business."

Jem's forkful of eggs froze halfway to his mouth. This would be the third night in a row Pa had not eaten supper with the family. *I have to ask him. I have to know.* He took a deep breath and blurted, "Your new sheriff job, Pa. It's temporary, right? I mean, just until they find somebody permanent?"

Pa shook a generous amount of pepper on his eggs before answering. "Why would you think that?"

Jem shrugged. Every time he watched Pa head to town on sheriff business, he wanted to run after him and beg him to stay home. Spring had brought a new rush of strangers to town. Many were hiring on at the Midas mine, but some just loafed and caused more than the usual trouble. Pa seemed to be gone from the ranch more than he was home.

"Well," Jem tried to explain, "instead of being a part-time sheriff, it's more like you're a full-time sheriff *and* a full-time rancher. You work hard all day and then break up fights and round up riff-raff half the night."

Ellie looked up in eagerness. Even Nathan seemed mildly interested in what his uncle would say. *At least, he's chewing slower than usual,* Jem thought. *Probably watching to see if Pa will swoop down on me like a hungry hawk and put me in my place.*

Pa set the pepper down. "The new jail's been broke in, that's for sure," he said with a chuckle. Then his look turned serious. "Son, I'm going to say this only once, so listen carefully. I almost turned down the offer of sheriff. It's a big job. And you're right: it's not the safest profession in town—or any place for that matter. But I thought long and hard about it; I even prayed about it. When a man feels he's got a call straight from the Good Lord to do something, well"—his voice grew quiet—"he's just got to do it."

Jem ducked his head. "I reckon that means it's not temporary?"

"You reckoned right," Pa said and went back to eating. When breakfast was over, he stood up and dropped his napkin on the table. "Delicious breakfast, Rosie, but I'd best get started on my day. It's gonna be a long one." He headed for the back porch, then turned and gave Jem a wink. "Say howdy to Strike for me, and pan us a fistful of gold nuggets today, ya hear?"

"I sure will!" At least Pa hadn't told him he was wasting time on a played-out gold claim. Jem grinned. He felt a little better, but not much. He couldn't shake the feeling that being a sheriff had to be the worst job in the West. *But I can't argue with Pa, and with God besides.*

Jem flew through the rest of his chores in record time. He was pleased to see that Nathan had managed to do his share with less than his usual clumsiness. *He's learning,* Jem thought happily. *This might turn out to be a good summer, after all.* He stuffed his gold pouch into his back pocket, snatched up his gold pan, and went outside to brush Copper.

Ellie ran up just then with a gold pan tucked under her arm and a lunch pail in her hand. "Let's hurry before Aunt Rose finds us more chores."

"Where's Nathan?" Jem asked. He tossed the brush aside, handed Ellie his gold pan to keep for him, and hoisted her up on Copper.

"Right here," Nathan called, running out the back door. Like Ellie, he was carrying a beat-up gold pan. He let Jem boost him up on Copper, then scooted backward to give Jem room.

Just then, Nugget bounded up, whining and circling the horse, tail wagging. He gave a short bark and looked up at Jem, who was climbing up on the horse. "Yeah, you can come." Jem sat up and gripped the reins. "But you better not sniff out any skunks." He nudged Copper into a trot.

Copper laid his ears back but gave no other sign that carrying three young riders was any more work than carrying two—or one. He walked along the road to town and down Main Street at a steady *clip-clop.* Swirls of dust rose behind Copper's hooves. It was hard to believe the street had been thick with mud a short six weeks ago.

From around the corner, a small figure dressed in black suddenly emerged, pushing a wheelbarrow overflowing with supplies. He glanced up from under his broad Chinese hat and grinned. "Hello, Jem."

Jem waved a greeting but didn't stop to pass the time with his friend Wu Shen. He was in a hurry to get out of town before his school chums saw him. He'd had enough teasing about being the sheriff's kid to last him a year.

Pa promised the teasing and mean-mouth comments would die down as soon as the town got used to the new way of doing things. Jem wasn't so sure. He nudged Copper into a trot to avoid meeting any more kids and turned the corner that led out of town and onto the path to Cripple Creek.

Ellie kept up a constant stream of chatter about the finer points of panning for gold. "And the most important thing," she finished, "is to make sure you're not in a hurry. If you swish the pan around too fast, the gold spills out with the gravel and dirt. Then you gotta start all over again."

"I know," Nathan said impatiently. "You don't have to tell me. I read all about it in a book. Sounds easy as pie. I betcha I find gold the very first time."

Jem snorted. "There's a big difference between reading about how to pan for gold and actually panning it. It takes a lot of practice and a lot of—"

"You'll see," Nathan interrupted. "I'm going to find the most." He took a deep breath and began singing off-key, *"I come from Massachusetts with a wash pan on my knee. I'm goin' to California, the gold dust for to see . . ."*

On and on Nathan bellowed, through endless verses about San Francisco, gold lumps, draining rivers dry, and pockets full of gold. *". . . so brothers, don't you cry!"*

"You're gonna be crying pretty quick if you don't put a plug in it," Jem warned his cousin. "What if somebody hears that nonsense?" He glanced around, didn't see any of his friends chasing after them, and kicked Copper into a lope.

Nathan gasped. He clutched his gold pan and hung on

so tightly that Jem could hardly breathe. It was a small price to pay to shut his cousin up.

"Just blamed foolishness," Jem muttered. Five minutes later, he urged Copper over the last hill overlooking the Coulters' claim alongside Cripple Creek. He shaded his eyes against the late morning sun and yanked the horse to a stop.

Something was dreadfully wrong.

⊰ CHAPTER 11 ⊱

Dry Diggings

Ellie reached over Nathan's shoulder and poked her brother in the back. "Where . . . where'd the creek go, Jem?" Her question was barely above a whisper.

Jem didn't answer. Stretched out from east to west—as far as he could see—what little was left of Cripple Creek trickled past. A few worn-out-looking miners were lifting shovelfuls of dirt and gravel into buckets, gunny sacks, and rough-hewn wheelbarrows. It was no wonder the men looked exhausted. Jem knew that every shovelful of dirt scooped from the creek bed would have to be hauled a mile away to Two Bit Gulch. There, the load could be washed to find whatever gold might be hidden in the dirt.

So much work for so little gold!

Ellie poked him again. "Jem? I asked—"

"I heard you," Jem said. "I don't know where it went."

He sat on Copper and tried to remember a time when the creek had looked like this. *Never*, he decided. Not even in the heat of the hottest August had Jem ever seen Cripple Creek flow like the narrow ribbon of brown it was today. Sure, the creek was never deep, and it ran a little low during late summer, but it had never run dry.

Dry Diggings

"Last time we were here, the creek was icy cold and running strong. What happened?" Ellie asked.

"Maybe it was a drier spring than we thought," Jem said.

Nathan scratched behind his ear and gave a half-smile. "I guess it's just like that song, *I'll drain the rivers dry.*"

"This isn't a river, so don't go on about some dumb ol' song," Ellie snapped as she dismounted.

"Same difference," Nathan said with a shrug. He tossed his gold pan to the ground and slid off the horse. Immediately, Nugget reached out and licked Nathan's hand. He pushed the dog away. "Does this mean we won't be panning for gold today?"

Jem ignored his cousin's question. Slowly, as if in a dream, he dropped to the ground beside Copper and tied him to the nearest tree limb. Then he headed down the low hill and onto the narrow strip of land that marked the Coulter claim. Shaking his head, he surveyed what was left of the creek.

Ellie and Nathan followed and stood next to him.

"No, Nathan," Jem finally said. He planted his hands on his hips and let out a long, frustrated breath. "We won't be panning for gold today or any other day. Not unless you've got a mind to haul the creek bed all the way to the stream in Two Bit Gulch." He shuddered at the thought. Hauling dirt was backbreaking work.

"Is that what those fellows are doing?" Nathan pointed to the handful of miners crouched over the stream bed with sacks and shovels.

Jem nodded, then glanced upstream. "I wonder where Strike is."

The old man's claim was littered with tent stakes, broken shovels, sardine cans, empty bottles, and a threadbare blanket. His coffee pail lay on its side next to the circle of blackened stones that marked the campfire. By the look of things, Strike had not tended his camp for some time.

"That's really disgusting," Nathan remarked.

Jem was forced to agree. Strike never worried about thieves. Not even the most desperate prospector looking for a grubstake would want what Strike left lying around. "Anything Strike values is tied to the back of Canary," he said.

Nathan looked confused.

"Canary is his burro," Jem explained.

Nathan laughed. "What a dumb name for a donkey."

"It's a *perfect* name." Ellie jumped to Strike's defense. "It's short for Mountain Canary, which is what folks call a prospector's burro. You should hear him 'sing.' His *hee-haw* is almost as loud as that ol' stamp mill. Canary is the most sure-footed animal around these parts. Smart too."

"Don't forget ornery, Ellie," Jem added with a sudden grin. "And stubborn. Canary's always running off. Strike spends more time looking for his donkey than he does looking for gold." He shaded his eyes toward the east. "I wonder where those two are."

"Probably looking for a new claim," Ellie said. She made a face at the prospector's current piece of ground. "Unless the creek starts flowing again, Strike won't be panning here."

"Neither will we." Jem crossed to Strike's claim and crouched beside the now-dead fire. "Cold as a grave," he said, brushing the ashes from his hands. He rose. "It doesn't make sense that Strike would be gone long enough to let his fire go out. He's mighty attached to his coffee. Besides," Jem added thoughtfully, "Strike and me . . . well, we're partners. He would've told me if he wanted to go off prospecting. Pa let me go with him last summer."

"We haven't been out here for over a month," Ellie reminded him. "Strike most likely got tired of waiting for his *partner* to show up."

Ellie was right. Jem had not been near Cripple Creek since the day they'd played hooky from school. He'd even rounded up his few frogs from Willow Spring rather than tramp all the way out to the swamp above the creek.

"Even if I couldn't pan for gold, I should have come by," Jem said. He made a fist and pounded it into his palm. Regret filled him. "I should have checked on Strike. He probably knows why the creek is running low. He knows everything about the gold diggings."

Jem paused, trying to decide what to do. The whole day would go to waste if he didn't get a chance to find some color, and he sure didn't want to go back to the ranch. Not yet, anyway. Aunt Rose probably had a new list of chores waiting. She could find extra chores quicker than Ellie could find frogs.

"Maybe the miners know where Strike went," Ellie said. "Let's ask 'em." She didn't wait for Jem to agree, but took off running along the creek bank. "Yoo-hoo!" she called, giving the men a friendly wave. Nugget bounded after her.

A couple of men glanced up when Ellie ran toward them, then went back to their digging and sack-filling without greeting her. The brush-off didn't seem to bother Ellie. She just tried farther upstream.

By the time Ellie found a miner willing to talk to her, Jem and Nathan had caught up. Nathan stood red-faced and hunched over, with his hands on his knees and sucking in air. "I . . . I told you to slow . . . down," he panted.

Jem hid a smile and turned to listen to the miner.

"Ain't seen that old-timer for a couple o' days," No-luck Casey was telling Ellie. He was up past his ankles in mud and gravel, scooping the creek bottom into a rickety wheelbarrow. He didn't stop digging to chat, but he seemed happy to pass the time while he worked. Beads of sweat dotted his balding head.

Jem wondered how No-luck planned to roll his wheelbarrow up the embankment with such a heavy load, but he didn't ask. "Do you know why the creek's dried up so early?" he asked instead.

No-luck swiped his forehead with a muddy hand and dug his shovel into the creek bed. "Nope. It's been runnin' lower and lower the past few weeks. Then it just up and quit altogether a week or two ago. I don't mind so much. Found a bit o' color yesterday. Maybe my luck's changing." He paused and grinned. "Ain't nothin' totally bad without some good to it, Jem. The sun'll dry up this mud soon. Dry diggings is easier to pack around than wet diggings."

Jem smiled back. Next to Strike, No-luck Casey was the friendliest, most easygoing prospector Jem knew. He was just about the poorest one too. Casey hadn't earned the name "No-luck" by accident. He usually prospected alone, on account of nobody would team up with him. Nobody wanted a broken arm, or a headful of lice, or smashed tools . . . or any other bad luck. One former partner had slipped and fallen into a ravine, losing his life.

Jem liked No-luck and hoped his luck had indeed changed, but right now he was worried about Strike. "Maybe he told you where he was off to?" he asked hopefully. It was unlikely that No-luck Casey knew. Most prospectors were closed-mouthed about their activities. Claims could get jumped because of a miner's loose tongue.

No-luck scooped another shovelful of dirt into the wheelbarrow and straightened up. "Nope. Didn't say a word."

Jem sighed and turned to go.

"But"—No-luck jerked his chin toward the mountains— "I did see Strike and that burro of his heading upstream the other day." His dirty face cracked a smile. "Everybody up and down Cripple Creek could hear his gear banging and that critter braying."

He lifted the handles of his wheelbarrow and gave it a push. It moved an inch. Jem knew it would be a long trip to Two Bit Gulch. "He could've gone to see why the creek stopped flowing," No-luck said. "It'd be just like the old fool. He's got more curiosity than what's good for him."

Jem thanked the miner and picked his way over the rocks and boulders until he reached the top of the creek bank. Then he sat down and watched No-luck navigate his wheelbarrow through the muddy channel and toward a spot along the bank where it was not so steep.

However, Jem was not interested in seeing if the miner could get the wheelbarrow out before it overturned on him. He was thinking—hard. *Strike's been gone for a couple of days. I wonder if he's all right. Sure he is,* he told himself. *He's prospecting. That's all.*

"We should go look for him," Ellie said, breaking into Jem's thoughts. She sat down and rested her chin on her knees.

Like always, Ellie seemed to know what Jem was thinking. "He's off prospecting," he said.

"Maybe. Maybe not." Ellie glanced up as Nathan plopped down beside them, then she turned back to Jem. "I bet you're just as curious about why the creek's dried up as I am. Even if we don't find Strike, it would be a nice ride and—"

"And something to do this afternoon," Nathan broke in.

Jem and Ellie turned and stared at their cousin.

"Hey," Nathan said, "I don't want to go back to the ranch any more than you do." He pushed aside a hank of pale hair that had fallen over his eyes. "Mother and Uncle Matthew don't expect us home until supper."

Jem looked at his cousin with a sudden sliver of respect. Did Nathan actually want to follow the creek into the untamed, tree-covered hills? So far, their cousin had not ventured farther on the ranch than the privy out back. He seemed more comfortable walking along the boardwalk in town than picking his way along a trail in the foothills.

"You *do* know that following the creek will take us up

toward the high country, right?" Jem said. "Ravines and pine forests, no real path to follow, no—"

"We might run into wild animals," Ellie added, eyes gleaming. "Maybe a rattlesnake or a bobcat or even a—"

"Are you trying to scare him, Ellie?" Jem burst out, jumping up. "You know we can't leave Nathan behind and go off by ourselves. Now, keep quiet." He turned to Nathan. "I just want you to know that it's no stroll down a boardwalk. But don't let Ellie's silly talk keep you from coming."

Nathan stood up to join Jem. "I'm not scared. Cautious, maybe," he said, glancing down at Ellie. "But not scared. Besides, I want to know where the creek went. Otherwise, I'll never get a chance to pan any gold. I'm game. The ride can't be *that* difficult. We're on a horse, after all."

Jem turned his gaze toward the Sierras, far away to the east. They would not begin to reach those mountains—not in an afternoon. But it would be quite a ride anyway, even on a horse. The hills around Goldtown rose quickly. *Let my cocky cousin find out for himself.*

"I want to find Strike," Jem said at last. He reached down and gave Ellie a helping hand up. "C'mon, let's mount up and get going."

⇥ CHAPTER 12 ⇤

A Rocky Path

How much longer do we have to stumble around in the
"middle of this dried-up ol' creek?" Nathan whined.

It wasn't the first question Nathan had asked since start-
ing out on their afternoon adventure. Jem had lost count of
the number of times his cousin had wanted to know where
they were going, how much farther it was, and what they were
going to do when they got there.

"I'm hot and I'm squished," Nathan complained. "And
I'm slipping all over this sweaty horse."

Jem gritted his teeth. *Hang it all! I should have left him back
at the claim. What was I thinking, bringing a tenderfoot along?*

Nathan's adventurous spirit had quickly drained away
when he discovered for himself that a trip into the hills was
not the same as a horseback ride through a Boston park.
The first few miles had been pleasant enough. They'd trotted alongside the grassy banks of Cripple Creek. Copper
lifted his head, shook out his mane, and easily carried his
riders. Nugget ran back and forth between the trees, sniffing
out a path. Although the creek was barely a trickle, it flowed
straight as an arrow between the rolling hills.

But it wasn't long before the terrain began to change.

The hills rose steeply, and the trees grew closer together. Cripple Creek cut through a high shale bank on one side. On the other side, underbrush forced the riders farther and farther away from the creek. Jem worried they might lose sight of their only sure path through the foothills.

So now they were picking their way carefully up the middle of the creek bed. Jem knew it wasn't called Cripple Creek for nothing. The sharp, unstable rocks could easily cause their horse to stumble or go lame. Copper didn't appear to like this choice of a trail any better than his riders did. Jem had to work hard to keep him moving. Time began to drag.

"When will we ever get out of this creek bed?" Nathan persisted.

Jem slapped at a pesky mosquito and yanked Copper to a standstill. Like Nathan, he was hot, sweaty, and thirsty. They had eaten their lunch long ago, and their one canteen would soon be empty. Jem pulled it off his shoulder and unscrewed the cap.

"I'll tell you what I told you an hour ago, Nathan," he said. "We're going to follow this creek until we find a reason it's running low, or see some sign of Strike, or both. You said you were game, so hush up or we'll dump you right here."

An idle threat. Jem would not leave Nathan alone, even if it was a simple matter to follow the creek back to the Coulter diggings. Not even a greenhorn city cousin could get lost. Or could he?

Jem glanced up at the cloudless, sapphire-blue sky. The sun had crept past high noon, but it still shone brightly at mid-afternoon. There was plenty of time before they had to turn around. He swallowed a gulp of warm, stale water and passed the canteen around. "If the sun drops too low, we'll hightail it back before it gets dark."

"Or we'll be in so much trouble we won't see past the ranch gate the rest of the summer," Ellie said.

Ellie was right about that. They had freedom to explore—Pa had made that clear to Aunt Rose—but woe to the Coulter kids if the sun set and they were missing from home. There were boundaries in town—too many to count—but Jem didn't like hanging around town anyway. He preferred to spend his free time panning for gold on the Coulter claim or joining Strike on a prospecting trip. Or like right now, when he could discover what lay beyond the next bend in the creek or over the next hill.

Jem leaned over and whispered in Copper's ear, "It's too bad Nathan has to be such a sissy and spoil the afternoon."

"Jem, look," Ellie whispered.

Jem sat up straight and glanced to where Ellie was pointing. On the low bank of the creek, off to his left, a small flock of wild turkeys scratched contentedly amidst the brush and golden grass under the trees. There were at least a dozen gobblers, and Jem's stomach rumbled at the sight.

"Wish I'd brought along the shotgun," he whispered. "Nothing's tastier than turkey." He cupped his hands to his mouth and let out a series of short, staccato clucks. One by one, the turkeys' heads jerked up from the ground. They stood stock-still, alert and listening. When Jem repeated the call, they answered.

He sighed and shook his head. "Aw, nuts. Look at 'em. Just waiting for me to take a shot. Dumb birds."

From upstream, Nugget wandered into sight. He was sniffing along the creek bank, nose to the ground, when his head went up. One glimpse of the turkeys sent the dog chasing after them, yipping wildly. In an instant, the entire flock scattered and disappeared into the woods.

"Nugget, no!" Jem shouted.

"He can't catch 'em," Ellie said, laughing. "He'll be back as soon as he figures that out." Then she sighed. "I like turkeys. They're just overgrown chickens. Might make good pets."

Jem forgot about Nugget for a moment. "Chickens and turkeys are good for only one thing, Ellie," he said. "Eating." But that didn't stop his sister from trying to make a pet of nearly every creature that crossed her path. She had names for all their chickens, the milk cow, and even an injured crow she'd tended last year. Only frogs seemed beneath her notice. *Good thing,* Jem thought, *or she might refuse to let the hoppers go to the café.*

The thought of Ellie trying to make a pet of a wild turkey made Jem think of the other wild animals roaming the woods. Ellie had been right when she'd warned Nathan. They could easily run into something more dangerous than a few turkeys.

"I'm glad we brought Nugget," he told himself. Then he yelled, "Nugget, get back here!"

As usual, it looked like the golden dog had a mind of his own. Jem could hear him barking from a long way off. *Still chasing those gobblers!* He raised two fingers to his lips and gave a long, shrill whistle.

No response.

"He's probably chasing those turkeys clear to Nevada," Ellie said. "Let's keep going. He'll catch up."

Jem clucked to Copper and nudged him along. From behind, he heard Nathan whisper, "Good riddance." Then the boy yelped and mumbled a quick apology.

Jem grinned. Ellie must have given Nathan a good pinch. He knew he should scold his sister, but it wouldn't do any good. Besides, their cousin deserved that pinch. His whining was getting on Jem's nerves. *This is the last time I take Nathan anywhere,* he promised himself.

Just then, Copper sidestepped to avoid a rock and stumbled. "Easy, boy," Jem said, pulling back on the reins. He felt Nathan slipping and gripped his knees tighter against Copper's sides. "Hold still, fella. You'll be—"

"Jem!" Ellie cried out. She and Nathan slipped farther off the horse. Jem tried to keep his seat, but it was no use. Nathan held onto his suspenders like a drowning man, pulling Jem down with him.

Thud! Jem gasped in pain. There was not enough water to cushion his fall—just a clear trickle that did nothing to dull the burning ache in his shoulder and left leg. Slowly, he sat up and looked around for their horse. Copper, free of his riders, had lost no time getting out of the rocky creek. He stood on the low bank, swishing his tail and tossing his head as if to say, "I'm not going back in there."

Jem agreed. He should have taken the hint the other times Copper had stumbled. It had been a warning Jem had not heeded. *Now*—he grimaced as he gingerly moved his arm—*I'm paying for it.*

Nathan's howls split the air, and Jem turned his attention to the other sorry figures sprawled on the rocks. Ellie was sitting up, her arms wrapped tightly around her knees. Her face was pale, and a large scrape showed red on one cheek, but she wasn't crying. Nathan shrieked loudly enough for the both of them.

He cries louder than a girl! Jem thought in disgust. "Ellie? You all right?"

Ellie nodded, blinking back tears. "I . . . I landed on top of Nathan. That's probably why he's yelling. He took most of the hurt."

Jem immediately felt sorry for pouncing on Nathan in his thoughts. He hurried over and laid a calming hand on his cousin's shoulder. "If Ellie fell on top of me, I'd be yelling too," he said, trying to lighten the mood. "Must've hurt somethin' fierce. Let me give you a hand up and we'll see if anything's broken."

Thankfully, Jem found nothing wrong with Nathan other than a deep, painful-looking scratch on his arm, and what would soon become a number of large, dark bruises. *Thank you, God,* he breathed silently. *This could have been bad.*

Jem helped Ellie and Nathan up onto the embankment. Then he rounded up Copper and tied him to a nearby manzanita bush. "I think we've gone far enough," he admitted. "Soon as you feel like it, we'll head back."

Nathan nodded and made no comment. Neither did Ellie, which was unusual. She wasn't one to give up up quite so easily. *She must hurt more than she's saying,* Jem decided.

Nugget's incessant barking reminded Jem that he couldn't leave his dog behind. "Nugget!" he yelled again and again, whistling between shouts. "Come on, boy! We're going home."

A few minutes later, Nugget emerged from between the trees. He had stopped barking—at last—and his tail was whipping back and forth. In his mouth, he held something brown and bloody. It looked like part of a turkey.

Jem slapped a hand against his forehead. "What have you done? Drop it, boy."

Nugget obediently trotted over and dropped his catch at Jem's feet. Then he backed up and sat down, tongue hanging out. Jem didn't want to look at the sorry remains of what had once been a large, splendid bird, but he couldn't help it. He glanced down at his feet and gasped.

It was not a turkey.

⊰ CHAPTER 13 ⊱

A Terrible Discovery

Jem's gasp brought Ellie and Nathan over at a run. They stared down at the "prize" Nugget had brought back, but no one touched it. Finally, Jem picked up a short stick and squatted beside the brown and bloody something. He worked the stick under the object and carefully lifted it to eye level. "It's a slouch hat," he said, examining it on all sides. "Not part of a turkey."

Ellie let out a sigh. "That's good."

Jem nodded. The discovery should have made him happy. Nugget had not ravaged a turkey after all. It was just an old, discarded hat—something only a dog would sniff out and find interesting enough to bring back. *Toss it aside and get going,* he thought.

Then Jem paused, and a different, troubling thought began to swirl around inside his head. He couldn't shake it loose. *There's something not right about this hat.*

"*Was,*" Nathan said just then. "It *was* a slouch hat. Now it's just a bloody mess." He wrinkled his nose.

Jem dropped the stick and jumped to his feet. His heart raced. "It's *fresh* blood all over this hat, not old, dried-up blood. See how bright red it is? This is recent." He knelt

91

down and peered closer. An invisible fist slammed into his stomach. "This could be Strike's hat," he whispered, looking up at Ellie and Nathan.

Ellie sucked in her breath. "Oh, no!" She took two steps backward, as if the hat might reach out and grab her. Then she whirled on Nugget. The dog still sat in place, clearly waiting for the praise due him for fetching such a magnificent trophy. "Where did you get this hat, Nugget?"

Nugget whined.

"Yes, yes, you're a good dog." She scratched behind his ears and crouched next to him. "But you have to show us where you got the hat."

Jem picked up the stick—with the slouch hat still hanging off one end—and took it to Nugget. Sometimes when Nugget brought back a raccoon or a possum, Jem convinced him to go after another of the varmints by saying, "More, Nugget!" However, more often than not, his dog brought back something entirely different.

Jem never knew for sure what Nugget might do next. He wasn't exactly reliable. But Jem had to try. He dangled the slouch hat under his dog's nose.

Nugget sniffed the hat and looked at Jem. His tail made a swishing noise as it fanned the grass and leaves.

"More, Nugget!" Jem commanded sternly. He was not playing today. This could be a matter of life or death.

In a flash, Nugget took off between the pine trees.

"Please, God," Jem prayed aloud, "make Nugget understand what I want this time. Don't let him rustle up a skunk instead."

"Amen!" Ellie yelled. She leaped up. "C'mon, Jem. Let's get Copper and go after him."

Nugget yapped in the distance, beckoning the kids to follow, but Jem held his ground. He needed to think things through. They didn't dare wander too far from the creek bed—their only sure path home. The afternoon was trickling away, and he had no desire to be caught out in these woods after dark. Besides, Pa expected him to watch out for Ellie and Nathan. Rushing madly after a dog was the height of foolishness, no matter how anxious Ellie was to get going. *It might not be Strike,* he reasoned. *Just a raggedy hat left behind on some old, abandoned claim.*

But the longer Jem looked at the slouch hat, the more convinced he became that it belonged to his friend and partner. Even if the hat didn't belong to Strike, the fresh blood came from *someone . . .* someone who might need help.

"Jem! Let's go!" Ellie had untied Copper from the brush and was jamming the reins into his hands.

"All right," Jem said, "but we can't ride. We need to mark the trail as we go, so we don't get lost. And"—he glared at Ellie—"we go only for as long as I say, and we keep the creek in sight the best we can. Agreed?"

"Agreed," Nathan muttered. He looked like he didn't want to go at all.

Ellie nodded her eagerness and ran ahead. If she disagreed with Jem about his instructions, she was keeping it to herself. "I'll tie you up and haul you back if you don't do what I tell you!" he yelled after her.

"With what?"

True enough. They'd ridden Copper bareback. The coil of rope Jem was threatening Ellie with hung from his saddle— the saddle back home in the barn.

Roasted rattlesnakes! Sisters can sure be a bother.

Jem chirruped at Copper and led him after Ellie, toward the sound of Nugget's barking. Nathan shuffled along behind his cousins, one hand gripping the horse's chestnut mane. As they trudged up a steep slope, Jem found a clump of low-lying manzanita and whacked at the branches with his pocketknife. He scattered them on the path, then smiled.

The ground was soft, and Copper was leaving a clear trail of hoofprints behind. Feeling better about not getting lost, he quickened his pace.

Ten minutes later, they stood at the top of a small ridge. Jem glanced around to get his bearings. To the southwest, he could see the outline of the creek. It was easy to follow the line of leafy trees and underbrush that hugged the creek on both sides. He even recognized where the three of them had left the creek bed. A high shale bank on the far side of the stream was partially visible between the tall pines that covered the hillside.

Nugget soon joined them, whining and circling their legs. A red bandana hung from his mouth. Jem took the piece of cloth and whooped. "This is Strike's. I've seen it plenty of times." He threw his arms around Nugget and hugged him tight. "Good dog," he said, ruffling his fur. Then he stood up. "More, Nugget!"

Nugget gave an excited bark and led Jem, Ellie, and Nathan along an open path between the trees. Another ten minutes brought them to a small, rocky clearing, where their dog was hanging over a bundle of red, brown, and black rags.

"It's Strike!" Jem shouted. He threw Copper's reins around a stubby pine tree and tore across the clearing at a dead run. His heart slammed against the inside of his chest like a hammer. "He's gotta be all right. He's just gotta be!" He heard the pounding footsteps of Ellie and Nathan behind him, trying to keep up.

Jem sank to the ground beside the old prospector. Strike lay sprawled out on his stomach, as still as death. His shoulder-length hair was matted with blood, both dried and fresh. A deep gash sliced the side of his forehead. *How long has he been like this? One day? Two? More?*

Ellie whimpered. "Is he . . . is he . . . ?"

"No!" Jem whirled on her. "He's not." Neither one spoke

the dreaded word aloud. Ellie might be thinking it, but Jem refused to believe Strike-it-rich Sam could be dead.

"How can you be sure?" Nathan stood a few yards off, keeping his distance. His face was drained of color. He stared at his cousins and the injured man.

"I just am," Jem said. But he *wasn't* sure. Not really. There was no outward sign that Strike was alive. He didn't move, and Jem could not tell if his friend was even breathing.

There was one way to find out. Taking a deep breath to steady his shaky hands, Jem bent closer. He gingerly pressed an ear against the old man's back and listened. A faint *thump, thump, thump* rewarded his effort. "He's alive." Jem sat back and sagged in relief. "Thank you, God."

At this good news, Ellie surged forward. She fell to the ground beside her brother and exclaimed, "He looks bad off. How do you suppose it happened?"

"It doesn't matter how it happened," Jem said, recovering from his initial shock. His thundering heart was slowly returning to normal, but the twisting in his gut told him this day was far from over. He looked up. "There's plenty of daylight left. We have to get Strike back to town, so Doc Martin can fix him up."

"Oh, sure," Nathan burst out, "easy as pie." He slumped to the ground and let out a long, uncertain breath. "How are we supposed to do *that?*"

Jem gave Nathan a furious look. "I don't know yet, but first things first." He took the bandana he was still clutching and pressed it against the gash in Strike's head. "Nathan, get over here."

The tone in Jem's voice propelled Nathan to his feet. He hurried over and dropped to his knees beside Jem. "What?"

"Hold this firmly against the cut, while I find something to tie it on with." Much to Jem's relief, Nathan did what he was told.

Jem quickly fished his knife from his pocket and beckoned Ellie over. "Let me have a strip of your hem for a wrapping."

"You can have my whole skirt if you want it," Ellie offered.

"No," Jem said, giving her an encouraging smile. "I just need a narrow piece." He snatched the edge of Ellie's skirt, sliced it through with the knife, and then ripped it all the way around. "I hope Aunt Rose doesn't give me what-for, seeing as I just ruined your only everyday dress."

"Pa won't let her scold you," Ellie said. "Not if my dress helps save Strike." She laid a hand on Jem's arm and pleaded, "It will, won't it, Jem? Once the bleeding stops, he'll be all right, won't he?"

Jem wasn't sure, but he nodded anyway. He hoped it didn't turn out to be a lie. "He'll be fine. Nathan, lift up his head."

Jem worked quickly to tie the strip of cloth around Strike's head, then sat back on his heels. Nathan gently lowered the prospector's head to the ground.

Without warning, Strike let out a low, agonized moan. His eyelids fluttered open. "W-w-water," he whispered. Nathan leaped away as if stung.

Jem fell backward in surprise but quickly recovered. "Strike, it's me, Jem. We have to turn you over so you can drink. We'll be as gentle as we can."

A slight movement from Strike looked like a nod, so Jem waved Nathan over to help. Together, the boys carefully turned the prospector onto his back. His head lolled to one side, and he groaned. Blood had seeped through parts of his flannel shirt and showed on one trouser leg.

Jem caught his breath at the sight. "He must have taken quite a fall. I hope nothing's broken." He yanked the canteen off his shoulder and fumbled to get the cap off. Then he gently raised the old man's head so he could drink. "Here's water. Take little sips."

Strike tried to swallow, but most of the water trickled down his chin. He coughed. "S-so . . . tired." His eyes closed.

"We're taking you home," Jem told him. "But we have to get you up on Copper. If we help, can you stand?"

The old prospector seemed to rally what strength he had and tried to sit up. Then he sagged against Jem. "I can't, boy. Hurts too much. Gotta . . . rest . . ." His voice trailed off, and he lost consciousness. Jem lowered him to the ground and sat back. *What now?*

"Somebody should go for help," Nathan said.

Jem frowned. Who could go? Nathan? He'd probably lose his way before he reached the creek. Ellie? She wouldn't get lost, but it would be dusk by the time she got home, and Strike would have to spend another night up here. *And I can't go. I can't leave Nathan and Ellie out here alone.*

"No," he said. "There's not enough daylight to get to town and back. We'll have to get Strike up on Copper somehow."

Nathan looked at Copper, munching on the sparse grass near the tree where Jem had tied him. Then he looked at the unconscious figure lying on the ground. "I can't lift an unconscious man up on a horse. Besides, he doesn't look so good. A trip like that might kill—"

"Strike's not very big," Jem insisted. "We can do this if we work together. Someone can sit on Copper and keep Strike from sliding off." He turned to Ellie. "Go get the horse."

Ellie shot to her feet and sprinted to the edge of the forest. Jem watched her go. He could tell by the way she tore at the reins and yanked on Copper that she was scared.

"Now what?" she asked when she returned, her eyes bright with unshed tears. Copper snorted and tossed his head.

Jem looked up, as if seeing his horse for the first time. Immediately, his plans crashed. Close up, Copper looked taller than his fifteen hands. Strike might weigh only a little more than Jem, but Copper's back was a long way up. *Even if we somehow get him up there, how will we keep him from slipping off? He's as weak and limp as a newborn calf.*

Annoyed with himself for not thinking clearly, Jem had no choice but to admit his cousin was right. Strike had a better chance of living if he stayed here, even if it meant another night out in the open. *But I won't leave him alone!* Jem rose. "You're right, Nathan."

Nathan gaped at Jem. "I am?"

Jem nodded. "Strike's too weak." He brought Copper around and handed Nathan the reins. "You and Ellie have to go for help. There's plenty of daylight left, so you should have no trouble getting home before dark. I'll stay with Strike. I have matches, and there's plenty of dead wood around. I'll build a fire." He reached down and gave Nugget a friendly rub. "I'll keep Nugget here to scare off any night critters."

While he talked to Nathan, Ellie's forehead wrinkled into a frown. Then she crossed her arms over her chest and glared at him. Jem sensed a clash coming on—a big one. He gave Nathan a boost up on Copper and pulled Ellie aside.

"Jem—" she began.

"Listen, Ellie," Jem whispered in her ear. "You gotta help me. Look at that greenhorn cousin of ours, sitting up on Copper. He doesn't know the way home, and he barely knows how to ride."

This was not completely true. Nathan could stay on a horse when he had a mind to. He didn't like to fall off any more than Jem or Ellie did, so he'd applied himself to staying on Copper at all costs. Ellie had to go along with Nathan, but it would take all of Jem's big brother sweet-talking to convince her to do it.

Ellie glanced at Nathan and shrugged. "So?"

"You gotta make sure Nathan gets back to town without getting lost. If he falls off, you know how Copper can get away quicker than a ground squirrel heading for his hole.

Then Nathan'll never make it back to town." He put an arm around his sister and gave her a warm hug. "Will you do it? Keep Nathan from getting lost, I mean?"

Ellie looked at the ground. "I want to help take care of Strike."

"I know," Jem said. "You can help him best by not letting Nathan get lost." Ellie didn't answer, which was a good sign. Before she had a chance to really think it through, he led her to Copper and boosted her up behind Nathan. "Get going, you two."

Jem gave Copper a whack on his rump and sent them on their way.

⌐ CHAPTER 14 ⌐

Decisions, Decisions

Jem watched Ellie and Nathan urge Copper across the clearing. They soon disappeared over the ridge, and Jem was alone. Nugget, ears alert, whined and started after the horse.

Jem called him back. "We're staying here, Nugget. Might as well hunker down and accept it." He knew it would take quite a while for Ellie and Nathan to make the return trip down the middle of Cripple Creek. Hopefully, Ellie would soon recognize landmarks so they could leave the creek and make better time. But going as fast as they could, they would not reach the ranch before dusk. *What then?*

Would Pa gather help and set out after dark? Even with lanterns and torches, Cripple Creek's treacherous bottom might prove deadly to one of the searchers. Surely, Pa would not take such a chance, not even to save Strike's life.

Jem shuddered. He was no sissy, but there was something eerie and unsettling about all this open country—especially at night. He looked up into the late afternoon sky and wracked his brain trying to remember if he'd seen the moon recently. Even a crescent moon would be a friendly face tonight.

A soft moan and a rustling noise rescued Jem from his

dismal thoughts. He pushed aside the coming night and focused on the needs of his friend. Uncapping the canteen, Jem lifted Strike's head and offered him water. This time, he heard a steady gulping as most of the liquid slipped down Strike's throat.

"Thanks," Strike whispered. His eyes were two slits, but he focused on Jem and cracked a tiny smile. "Glad . . . ya found . . . me." It appeared to take all his strength to get those few words out.

"Don't talk," Jem said, squeezing Strike's hand. "I'm staying right here. Ellie and Nathan went for help. Don't you worry about a thing."

Strike coughed feebly and wagged his head. "No. You get on . . . home. Gotta . . . tell ya . . ." He gave a quiet sigh and closed his eyes.

Jem let go of Strike's hand and allowed himself a smile. The old man had awakened twice now. It was a miracle what a difference a little water made. He capped the canteen and gave it a shake. "Not much left in here. And who knows where I'll find more."

With the creek barely a trickle, it was unlikely Jem would find more water up here above Cripple Falls than down below. It was worth a try, however, but not before he'd gathered an armful or two of dry wood for tonight. He didn't need a fire for heat—late spring nights around Goldtown stayed warm—but a cheerful blaze would keep him from feeling completely alone in the dark while Strike slept.

Jem rose and looked down at his friend. He wished he could give him some relief from the sun burning down on his face. But it wouldn't be long before the sun slipped behind the treetops. Strike would have all the shade he needed then.

Jem set out for the edge of the clearing to look for dead branches and old pine needles. Dry needles would catch fire in no time. In these hills, no one worried that their wood might be too wet to burn well. Instead, the constant threat of fire kept folks careful to keep their campfires small and isolated.

It took Jem no time at all to collect a pile of branches and needles for the night ahead. He emerged from the woods with his last load, whistling the song Nathan had bellowed earlier that day about pockets full of gold. *I can't get that tune out of my head.*

Suddenly, he stopped. It looked like Strike was sitting up. His heart flew to his throat in joy. Just as quickly, it fell to his toes. Fear made him drop his bundle and rush over to where he'd left Strike and Nugget.

"Ellie!" he shouted, panting. "What happened? What's wrong? Where's Nathan?"

Ellie stood up and faced her brother. "Nothing's wrong. I did what you told me. I made sure Nathan got back to the creek without getting lost. He can—"

"What were you *thinking*?" Jem took hold of Ellie's shoulders and shook her. "You're supposed to go get help! I don't need you here. Do you know what Pa's gonna do to me when he sees you're not with Nathan?" His anger spent, he stepped back and let his arms fall to his sides. "Haven't you got any sense at all?"

Ellie stood her ground, but her lip quivered at her brother's words. When she spoke, it was barely above a whisper. "I planned to, Jem. I really did. But everybody knows it's easier for one person to ride bareback than two or three slipping around. We were working hard not to pull each other off. When we got to the creek, Nathan told me he could go faster on his own."

Jem's eyebrows shot up. "He did?"

Ellie nodded. "Took me by surprise. He got real bossy about it. Insisted he knew the way, once I got him back to the creek. Promised he'd go as fast as he could, but that"—Ellie huffed—"I was slowing him down."

Jem took a deep breath and got ready to yell some more. Pa would really, *really* be worried when he learned that Ellie was out in the hills all night. Then he let out his breath. It was too late. Nathan was long gone. Besides, his cousin was right. He could make better time alone. "Chalk one up for Nathan," Jem said, cracking a smile. "Under all our cousin's complaining ways, maybe he's got some real 'gold' in him when it counts."

He didn't want to admit it, but now that he'd simmered down he rather liked the idea of Ellie keeping him company tonight. *I can't let Ellie know that,* he told himself, *or she'll never listen to me again.*

"I dropped a load of wood right beyond that boulder," he growled, pointing. "Go fetch it. Then we can talk about finding some water to fill the canteen and how we're gonna last all night with no supper."

"Betcha I can last longer than you," Ellie said with a grin. Clearly, she saw right through her brother's growly voice and knew she'd been forgiven for coming back.

Jem couldn't help it. Try as he might, he could not keep from laughing. "Get going!"

The sun finally slid behind the tops of the pine trees, giving Strike, Ellie, and Jem relief from the late afternoon heat. But the shadows reminded Jem that night was coming, and they had little water, no food, and no shelter. "It's just for one night," he muttered, too low for Ellie to hear. "But it will be the longest night of my life. I bet I don't sleep a wink."

Ellie had cleared a spot and then laid a fire of dried grass, pine needles, small sticks, and large branches. All it needed was the strike of Jem's match. Around the fire pit, she had carefully placed a ring of stones, each one in its own special place.

Jem chuckled. Ellie sure knew how to amuse herself. He lay spread out on his back, gazing into the sky. If Strike was not in such need, and if he and Ellie were not stranded up here, Jem would have thoroughly enjoyed the peace and quiet. Only a faint clanging from the stamp mill reached this far into the hills; not a breeze rustled the tree tops.

He could not lie around much longer. Strike needed water. Now that Ellie was here, there was no excuse. She could stay with the old prospector while he checked the creek above Cripple Falls.

"Jem!" Ellie suddenly gasped. "Listen!" She jumped up and peered toward the mountains. "Hear that?"

Jem sat up and held his breath, listening. Breaking the afternoon silence came a sound he knew well. "It's Canary."

Ellie pointed into the woods leading toward the falls. "He's up there somewhere."

"I forgot all about him," Jem said, shaking his head. Canary's absence had crossed his mind earlier, but he'd been too busy worrying about Strike to pay attention to where the donkey might have wandered off to. Canary was not known for his loyalty.

A new thought propelled Jem to his feet. He brushed himself off and said, "Canary's packing Strike's supplies—food, water, mining tools. If I can catch him, we'll have plenty of water for Strike, and some supper too."

Ellie frowned. "I should go after him. He likes me best."

"He doesn't like anybody best— not even Strike," Jem said. "And I'm better at making him mind than you are."

Jem knew Ellie couldn't argue with that. Sometimes

Canary needed a sturdy stick across his hindquarters to make him move. Ellie's whacks were more like love pats. Canary usually just looked at her and laid his ears back when she tried to get him to go.

"I'll give Strike the last of the water, then go after Canary," Jem told her. "If I can't find him, I'll stop and see if there's any water above the falls. Then I'll come right back. You stay here and keep an eye on things." He cocked an ear and heard another bray. "Canary doesn't sound too far away. Wish he'd stuck around for once, instead of running off."

Ellie nodded her agreement and sat down next to Nugget. The dog lay sprawled out on his side, fast asleep. When Ellie touched him, his head snapped up and his tail thumped. "Nugget and I will take care of Strike while you're gone," she promised.

"Good idea." Jem smiled at her. "I won't be long." *It's about time you did something I told you,* he thought. He knew better than to say it out loud—not if he wanted Ellie to keep minding him. *Besides, you can catch more flies with honey than with vinegar.* Aunt Rose had told him that more than once during the past few weeks.

Jem gently lifted Strike's head and offered him the last few swallows from the canteen. The prospector opened his eyes and latched onto Jem's arm with a thin, clawlike hand. His lips moved, but no words came out. Instead, he slumped and lay still.

"He's sure upset about something," Ellie remarked. "Every time you give him water, he tries to talk. It's kind of creepy."

"He's probably delirious from pain or fever or thirst," Jem said. "He doesn't know what he's doing. Soon as we get him to Doc Martin, he'll be back to his old self." He shouldered the canteen and took a few steps toward the trees. Nugget rose to all fours.

"Stay here," Jem commanded. "Stay with Ellie."

Nugget barked once and sat down.

Amazing! Jem didn't know what to make of it—Nathan acting unafraid and going for help alone; Ellie agreeing to stay with Strike; Nugget obeying instantly. Jem felt pretty good as he waved to Ellie and jogged across the small clearing and into the woods. *Now, if only Pa would come over the rise right about now, this day would be perfect.*

Jem knew Nathan had not reached town yet. Pa would not be riding to the rescue any time soon. "It's up to me. All I have to do is keep Strike alive for one more night and keep Ellie from getting too scared of the dark." If he focused on what he had to do, maybe he would not be so frightened of the coming dark night himself.

One thing at a time, Jem reminded himself. Right now he needed to find that stubborn donkey and fill the canteen. He paused. Not getting lost would be a good idea too. He dug into his pocket for his knife and slashed at a few branches.

Hee-haw! Hee-haw! Canary's braying grew louder and closer.

Jem kept moving. He knew he was on the right track, but he had not expected to hike so far. Then he remembered that Canary's "singing" could be heard a long way off. He kicked a piece of deadwood. "He could still be half a mile away." Chasing an ornery burro through the foothills of the Sierras was the last thing Jem wanted to do. "A few more minutes, then I'll settle for finding a puddle in Cripple Creek. Ellie will get worried if I stay away too long."

Canary's braying came again. Since it came from the direction of the stream, Jem followed it. He quickened his pace, scurried up a gentle slope of pines, and suddenly came out at the top of Cripple Falls. The falls trickled over the twenty-foot drop, a mere dribble of their usual volume. That was plenty of water for Jem. He could creep out over the rocks and fill his canteen from the small pool just above the falls.

But Jem made no move to go after the water. Instead, he stared at a rough, wooden trough resting in place just a little farther up the creek. "What in the world?" he whispered.

A sudden desire to keep out of sight washed over Jem. He dropped to his knees behind some brush. Cautiously, he lifted his head above the bushes and studied the structure. It was a wooden trough—a flume, really—that stretched from the creek above Cripple Falls to out of sight beyond the trees on the other side of the creek.

Jem did not have to crawl into the flume to know what was in it. Water—a lot of it. Streams of water gushed through the seams between the flume's sections. Whoever had thrown together this flume had done so in a hurry. The builders did not seem to care how much water they wasted, so long as most of it reached its destination, wherever *that* was.

Jem didn't know where the flume ended, but he knew what it was for. A miner—or most likely more than one miner—was working a large gold claim nearby. As Jem's gaze followed the wooden trough running downhill, away from the creek, the pieces of the dry Cripple Creek "puzzle" fell into place.

"Why, those low-down skunks!" Jem clenched his fists. "They diverted the creek to wash their own gold." He was furious at whoever was stealing water from Goldtown's prospectors. Miners like Strike could barely make a living washing placer gold. *Without* water, it was impossible. Jem wanted to rush over and knock down a section of the flume. Instantly, the water would return to its rightful course and tumble over Cripple Falls again.

"Cool your heels," Jem ordered himself as he ducked behind cover. "That's a sure way to let those ruffians know something's up. Besides, I doubt bare hands would do much, even if the flume *is* a shoddy piece of work." He chewed on his lip and thought, *What to do? What to do?*

A loud *hee-haw* brought Jem's head up for another peek at the flume. He sucked in his breath at the sight of Canary just beyond the creek. He seemed to be standing next to the flume. Jem strained to get a better view. Canary was not just standing under the flume. He was tied to one of the supports, looking more miserable than any donkey Jem had ever seen. No one had bothered to relieve the poor beast of his pack. Jem doubted anyone had even fed or watered him.

Canary laid his ears back and brayed mournfully, as if pleading to be set free. Ten minutes stretched by while Jem sat hunched behind the manzanita and elderberry bushes, thinking. It all made sense now. "Strike must have found the flume and tied Canary up to keep him from running off. But he got caught." Someone had beaten up an old man and abandoned a helpless animal. It made Jem angry . . . and frightened. Somebody was stooping mighty low to keep their operation hidden.

He listened to Canary's braying and realized he would have to leave the donkey for now. As much as he wanted to free him—and take advantage of the supplies—he knew it would be foolish and risky. Canary was clear across the creek and out in the open. What if the miners were close by? It wouldn't take long to discover the donkey was missing. What then?

Yes, Jem decided, going back to camp was the only decision that made sense. "But water first." Prickles raced up and down his spine. Even that was risky, but he needed the water. "Then I'll hightail it back and wait for Pa. Ellie will have a fit if she finds out I left Canary, so I just won't tell her."

Jem yanked the canteen off his shoulder and headed for the pool of water just above the falls. It was slippery going, but he carefully picked his way over the rocks and dipped his canteen in the creek. It gurgled as it filled, and soon Jem was taking a long, satisfying drink. He capped the canteen, rose, then turned for one final glimpse of Canary.

And found himself looking right into the business end of a Colt .44 revolver.

⊰ CHAPTER 15 ⊱

Tied Up Tight

"*Bonjour, enfant.* Make no sudden moves."

Jem didn't intend to make any moves—sudden or otherwise. He stood frozen, his fingers curled around the strap of his canteen. Looking down at him from under familiar black eyebrows, Frenchy seemed taller than his six feet two inches. Jem felt like David standing much too close to the giant, Goliath. *And a canteen is no sling!*

Jem swallowed and said nothing. He could not have spoken even if he wanted to. His throat felt drier than dust. Jean-Claude "Frenchy" DuBois was the last person Jem expected to meet in the middle of nowhere. By now, the miserable claim jumper should have been miles away—maybe clear to Stockton or San Francisco—*not* within hanging distance of the town that had banished him and his partners weeks ago. If anyone saw them still lurking in the area, the miners' court would not be so forgiving.

Frenchy swept open his long, black overcoat and holstered the revolver out of sight. "Did I frighten you?" he asked with a grin. His teeth showed yellow and broken through his coal-black beard.

Jem wondered if a nod counted as a sudden move. He

110

decided to keep still and let Frenchy think he was just surprised. As long as he kept his hands from shaking, and his legs didn't turn to jelly, Jem might even believe it himself.

Frenchy reached out and gripped Jem's arm. It hurt plenty, but Jem's tight throat kept him from yelping. "I know who you are. You are the sheriff's son." Frenchy spat, as if the word *sheriff* left a bad taste in his mouth.

Which, Jem figured, it probably did. Frenchy had caused trouble in Goldtown for years. His banishment had been just a matter of time. No doubt the new sheriff—*uh, that would be Pa,* Jem thought bleakly—had been instrumental in making it happen a lot sooner.

It didn't look like Frenchy expected an answer, so Jem gritted his teeth against the pain in his arm, clutched his canteen, and stumbled along beside the giant. He was not surprised when they began following the flume downhill.

"I heard barking earlier," Frenchy remarked. "Thought maybe somebody found their way up here. Then I saw you nosing around, peeking out from behind the brush. Got your curiosity tickled, *oui?* Enough to blab about what you saw?"

Frenchy sure likes to hear himself talk, Jem thought.

"What are you doing up here?" Frenchy asked. When he received no reply, he squeezed Jem's arm. "Answer me, *enfant.*"

Jem didn't like being called a child in any language, but the pain loosened his tongue. "I'm just killing an afternoon," he said with a gasp.

"You hiked up here from town?"

Jem nodded.

Frenchy's black brows rose into his hairline. "That is a long walk for a boy! I think maybe you rode. Yet, I see no horse. So, I wonder . . . where is it?"

Jem gritted his teeth and focused on staying alert. He felt reassured to see that they were still following the flume.

The wooden trough was the best trail marker Jem could have hoped for.

"I think your horse is tied up someplace else," Frenchy rambled, yanking Jem to hurry him along. "Perhaps near that nosy old man—"

Jem's sudden intake of breath gave him away.

Frenchy nodded. "*Oui, oui,* I should have guessed. The old man is a friend"—he chuckled—"or should I say he *was* a friend? By now he has probably bled out from his accident."

Boiling hot rage drove every ounce of fear from Jem. He slammed his heels into the ground, twisted his arm, and wrenched free from Frenchy's grip. Before he could take three steps, though, the man was upon him. He pinned Jem's arms to his sides and lifted him in the air. The canteen went flying.

"You tried to kill him!" Jem shouted, kicking and thrashing.

"Maybe so," Frenchy said with a laugh. "But he was too nosy for his own good, poking around where he does not belong. No one would miss an old miner off prospecting."

"*I* missed him!" Jem wiggled and squirmed, but it was no use. Frenchy held him fast.

"Shut up and mind your manners." He dropped Jem to the ground and grasped a handful of dark hair. Jem winced. "The claim is just beyond those trees."

Anger could keep fear away for only so long. As Jem was led to the torn-up parcel of land Frenchy called a gold claim, dread washed over him. He looked around. The flume ended abruptly, spilling water into a long sluice box before it splashed down the hill in a newly gouged-out gully. Where the water went from there was anybody's guess.

A large mining hole took up a good portion of the ground just in front of Jem. He peeked over the edge and sucked in his breath. It was a deep hole, dark and dank. A windlass stretched across the top, supported by two posts.

Jem watched a rough-looking miner turn the crank on the windlass. A length of rope wound around a wooden cylinder, and a bucket of dirt and gravel began to slowly make its way up to the surface. As soon as the contents were dumped into a wheelbarrow, the bucket fell back into the hole. Jem stepped back, but not before catching a glimpse of two men at the bottom of the hole, picks in hand.

"We've pulled thousands of dollars of gold from that hole," Frenchy hissed in Jem's ear. "All we needed was water to wash it."

Thousands of dollars! Jem gulped. *A rich strike indeed.* He counted the number of men working the claim. Half a dozen at least. A nice little operation they had going here. No wonder they needed water. Hauling the diggings up the side of the hill to the creek would have been nearly impossible. Without water to wash the gold from the dirt, the claim was worthless.

Frenchy yanked Jem away from the mining hole and shoved him to the ground next to a campfire. A large, black pot hung from a tri-pod over the flames. In spite of his terror, Jem's stomach turned over in hunger. Whatever they had cooking in that pot sure smelled good! His mouth began to water.

Frenchy squatted beside Jem and gave him a smack across the head. It didn't hurt—much—but it sure got his attention. "What are we going to do with you, boy?"

The other miners shuffled toward the campfire. They formed a ring around the young intruder and glared at him. "I say we call it quits and hightail it outta here," one said. "This claim's playin' out, anyway. We're washin' only a quarter of what we were before. A couple more weeks and it'll be gone."

Frenchy scowled at the grime-encrusted miner. He obviously didn't want to leave *any* gold behind. "What about you, Jerky?" he asked the man nearest him. "You want out?"

Jerky scratched behind his ear. "I think it's too risky to stay now. Maybe nobody missed the old man, but I betcha they're lookin' for this kid." He spat a stream of tobacco juice into the fire. "We knew it couldn't last. Somebody was bound to get curious and come lookin' for a reason the creek dried up so soon."

"But not a snot-nosed *kid*!" Another miner cursed and kicked a rock. It went sailing across the fire pit. "Let's tie him up. We finish bringing out what's in the hole and get it washed. Then we pack up and head for Nevada at first light. I say we dump the kid in the hole on our way out. That'll keep him from blabbin' to his pa too quick."

Jem grew cold inside thinking about being trapped in the miners' hole. One way in. No way out. He dropped his head in his hands and took a long, deep breath. His thoughts turned into a desperate prayer for safety and deliverance . . . mostly for deliverance. *And please, God, don't let these skunks find Ellie. Maybe I can hold out 'til Pa finds me.* In spite of his prayer, clammy fingers of panic clutched his insides.

A swift kick to his leg brought Jem's head up. Frenchy stood above him, holding a length of rope. "You heard my partners. We cannot let you go. You understand, *oui*? Now, get up."

Jem slowly got to his feet. Half a dozen evil gazes bore into him, daring him to make a run for it; wanting an excuse to rough him up and keep him subdued. Jem took one last glance at the pot of grub he had no chance of eating. Then he let Frenchy haul him away from the fire and toward a row of trees at the edge of the claim.

In the distance, a new round of Canary's forlorn "singing" made Jem ask, "Why haven't you untied the donkey? It's cruel to keep him tied up out there."

Frenchy shrugged his indifference. "You should worry less about that *baudet* and more about yourself, *oui?* I will find a use for him sooner or later." Dangling the rope from his hand, he motioned Jem to the ground, then shoved him tightly against the trunk of a young pine. "Which is more than I can say about *your* usefulness." His beard split in an ugly grin.

Jem stiffened when Frenchy pulled his arms around the trunk. His shoulders felt like they were being wrenched from their sockets. He clenched his teeth against the searing pain but didn't make a peep. The scratchy rope bit into his wrists and made them burn. He wiggled his fingers to take the pressure off, but it didn't help. A pins-and-needles feeling slowly began creeping into his hands.

"*Au revoir,*" Frenchy said, ruffling Jem's hair. Then he was gone, back to the cheerful blaze a dozen yards away.

Jem did not return Frenchy's good-bye. Instead, he sagged against the tree trunk and tried to find a comfortable position. He no longer cared about escape. All he wanted was relief from the pain. His arms ached, his wrists and hands were asleep, and his left shoulder screamed at him. The bark of the pine tree jabbed him in the back. His stomach clenched into a knot tighter than the knots binding him to the tree.

Jem knew that by morning he would be unconscious

from the pain—or groggy from lack of sleep, on account of the pain. He didn't know which was worse. *I have to loosen this rope,* he determined. He clenched and unclenched his fingers. It did nothing to ease the rope's bite. It only made the pins and needles stab more viciously.

Jem stopped struggling and leaned his head back against the tree. Against his will, tears sprang to his eyes. The miners had tied him up and left him alone without another thought. They were too busy eating, drinking, and bringing up the last bucketfuls of gold from their hole to care about a frightened young boy tied up in the shadows just beyond their camp. In the morning, they would abandon him with as little conscience as they had when they left Canary tied up to starve.

All that mattered was the gold.

Over the years, Jem had seen gold fever infect plenty of men. It was scary to watch the miners fight and steal, driving themselves to near death as they struggled to strike it rich. They didn't let anyone stand in their way. They were a law unto themselves, and even the miners' court was not always effective. Whippings and banishments worked only part of the time. Hangings worked, but only as a last—and permanent—resort.

Thankfully, Jem had never suffered from the effects of gold fever. When the Coulter claim began to play out, Pa didn't drag his family to the next muddy gold camp, or to the one after that. Instead, he bought a ranch and set out to make a new life.

"Does that life mean taking a job as sheriff too?" Jem asked aloud. It was a new thought—one Jem was reluctant to admit to himself. "Maybe Pa became sheriff to make Goldtown a safer place for *us*—for Ellie and me, and Nathan and Aunt Rose. And all those others who are tired of letting folks run wild."

Jem's gaze turned to the dark shapes grouped around

the campfire. "Pa became sheriff to keep me safe from men like *them*," he whispered in sudden understanding. Stinging tears pricked his eyes. Of *course* Pa must know being a sheriff was dangerous! But he was willing to do the job anyway—for his family.

The sky began to darken. The pine's branches blocked Jem's view, but he could imagine the first stars of the night dotting the sky. Perhaps the moon would rise too. If so, Pa would not wait until morning. Shivers of hope raced up and down Jem's spine. "Please let there be a moon tonight," he whispered. "A full one, lighting up the whole sky."

Jem waited, but no moonlight turned the forest into shadows. The glow of the campfire soon became the only light Jem could see. His spirits drooped as the fire burned down. Occasional laughter told him the miners were drifting off. It was getting late.

Jem yawned. In spite of the constant burning in his arms and hands, he felt drowsy. Perhaps he could forget his pain and fear in sleep. His head lolled onto his chest.

Scratch, scratch . . . rustle.

Jem's eyes flew open. His head snapped up. Fear flooded his mind. Bobcat? Wolf? Bear? The miners had left him alone to be eaten by wild animals! He filled his lungs with air for a shout that would surely get their attention.

"Shhhh!" Ellie's hand clamped over Jem's mouth.

The shock of seeing his sister made Jem's heart race with hope and relief. Then dismay, terror, and red-hot anger took over. He was helpless to do anything about it, though. Ellie's hand still covered his mouth. He pierced her with a furious glare.

"You can yell at me later," Ellie whispered, removing her hand. "Do you have your knife?"

Jem nodded. "In my right pocket."

Ellie dug around in Jem's trouser pocket. She pulled the

knife out and snapped it open. Jem could barely make out her face. Night had fallen, black and heavy.

Without a word, Ellie slipped around to the back of the tree and began to cut her brother loose.

-⊰ CHAPTER 16 ⊱-

On the Run

Jem shook the pieces of rope from his wrists and staggered to his feet. He didn't waste time rubbing the feeling back into his arms and legs. Who knew when Frenchy or another miner might check up on their prisoner? He looked around. It was so dark that Jem could barely see three feet ahead.

Ellie whispered something, but Jem hushed her and grabbed her hand. He stumbled along as fast as he dared, away from the glow of the dying embers in the miners' camp.

They hadn't gone more than a dozen yards when something huge and black rose up in front of them. *Ooof!* The force of the impact slammed Jem backward. He clutched his shoulder and groaned. He hadn't seen that tree, and now he was paying the price for his haste. *How will we ever get away?* he wondered, sucking in deep breaths.

Ellie whimpered. Jem reached for her hand. "I'm fine," he told her quietly. "Nothing's broken. Let's try it again, but slower this time." He forced his voice to sound light, but Ellie probably saw right through his attempt to reassure her.

Jem clenched his jaw against the pain and carefully circled the tree. He was the big brother. He had to take charge, even though he was scared silly. He wished Pa was here. His father would make everything all right. *But Pa's not here! I have to keep Ellie safe until he comes for us.*

"L-let's go back to Strike," Ellie begged. She was shaking, in spite of the warm night. "We can follow the flume to the creek. The stars will give us a little light. Maybe the moon will come out too."

"We can't take the chance," Jem whispered. "We have to stick to the woods." Right now his only goal was to stay out of sight and get as far away from Frenchy and his ruffians as possible. Direction didn't matter, and deeper into the forest seemed like a good choice. He kept a tight grip on Ellie's hand and kept walking.

They crept cautiously through the woods, but it was impossible to avoid every hazard. Jem could not keep back his yelp of shock and dismay when he tripped over a fallen log and sprawled on the ground.

Ellie landed in a heap beside him. "Please, Jem," she sobbed, "let's find the flume. It'll take us straight to the creek. Please? I don't want to get lost."

Jem scooted over and sat down on the log to rest and think. Maybe Ellie was right. It was darker than a stack of black cats in the forest, and his aching shoulder reminded Jem of the dangers of being careless. There were worse things than trees to guard against. One false step in the dark, and they could easily find themselves falling into a deep ravine. Or becoming hopelessly turned around in the vast, wooded foothills.

"All right," Jem said at last. "Let's find the flume and head for the creek. Maybe the miners are asleep by now, or too drunk to bother checking up on me." He cocked his head and listened. Although he could see nothing in the dark, murky forest, he could hear the flume. The steady sound of splashing raised Jem's spirits. He squeezed Ellie's hand. "This way. Come on."

On the Run

Jem kept them creeping along for what he figured was about twenty minutes, although it felt more like an hour. Every few minutes, he stopped and listened for sounds of pursuit. He could hear nothing over the noise of the leaky flume. It was now their constant companion, a broad trail marker through the woods, even in the dark. The trees had been cut down to make room for the wooden trough, and the water splashed and gurgled past them in a friendly, familiar manner.

Ellie tripped, forcing Jem to stop and yank her to her feet . . . again. It was the third time she'd stumbled in the past ten minutes. Before he could take three steps, she slumped to the ground and refused to budge. "I'm tired."

"We can't stay here," Jem reminded her. "It's not safe. We haven't come very far, what with having to creep around like a couple of snails." He knew that Frenchy and the others would find them as soon as the sun came up. Worse, Ellie would be caught this time. "We have to keep moving."

There was no answer. Jem dropped to the ground. He wrapped his good arm around Ellie and gave her a little shake. "Hey, don't go to sleep."

Ellie laid her head against him. "I'm tired," she said, sniffing back tears. "And . . . and I'm scared. I want Pa."

"I know," Jem said. He wondered how long she'd been quietly crying. "Betcha he'll start out even before the sun comes up. He'll bring along deputies and plenty of lanterns and torches—enough to light up Cripple Creek so they don't slip and fall or lose their way."

Ellie rubbed her eyes. "You really think so?"

"You bet! And Nathan will be with them, of course. He'll show Pa just where we left the creek. Then they'll gallop up the hill, over the rise, and find Strike." He paused. The thought of his injured friend spending another night out in the open made Jem frown. "I hope Strike's all right."

"He's not alone," Ellie said. "I told Nugget to stay with him." She sniffed back her tears and took a deep breath. "All right, Jem, I'm ready. You can yell at me now for coming after you."

Jem laughed, in spite of his fear and worry. "I don't want to yell at you anymore, Ellie. I'm glad you showed up. How did you find me, anyway? You couldn't track me in the dark."

Ellie was quiet for a moment. Then she looked up. Jem could just make out her face. "I think . . . I think God helped me," she said softly.

"How's that?" Jem asked in surprise. He'd been praying plenty this evening, but he hadn't really thought much about *how* God would go about rescuing him.

"Strike woke up long enough to tell me about those men," Ellie explained.

Jem nodded. "Frenchy and the others. They caught Strike and hurt him bad."

"I was scared they'd catch you too," Ellie went on. She didn't sound sleepy any longer. "I had to come after you and warn you. God helped me find your trail. It wasn't hard. You left a pretty big one. I came out at the falls and saw the flume, but I didn't see you. I saw Canary, though. He's tied up to the flume!"

"I know."

"I crossed the creek bed and was gonna untie him when I saw your canteen on the ground. I got real scared then, 'cause I knew they must've caught you. So I hid in the woods and sneaked around until I saw you at their claim."

She began to cry. "There were so many of them! I . . . I watched Frenchy tie you up. I knew I couldn't help you 'til it was dark, so I waited and waited. And I prayed, 'cause I was scared they'd catch me too."

Jem fished around in his back pocket for a handkerchief. "Here, Ellie, use this." He squeezed her shoulders. "That was mighty brave of you, to leave Nugget behind and come on your own."

"I couldn't bring Nugget. You know how he is. He'd have gone after those low-down, nasty claim jumpers and got himself shot."

"You're right," Jem said. Nugget and strangers were not a good mix. More than once, Pa had to keep Nugget in check when unfamiliar guests visited the ranch.

Ellie blew her nose, but she didn't stop crying. "The . . . the only th-thing is," she stammered, "I c-couldn't . . . free Canary. I had to leave him and go after you first." Loud, wrenching sobs poured from her.

"*Shhhh!* Not so loud," Jem warned. "We don't know how far we've come, and sound travels a long way in these hills. They might hear you even over the noise of the flume."

Instantly, Ellie muffled her cries. "I forgot. But Jem? Can't we untie Canary and take him with us? Please?"

Jem choked back his astonishment. Here they were, hiding out in the woods from men who would toss them in a mining hole without a moment's thought, and all Ellie could think about was that donkey! "No, Ellie. I feel sorry for him, really I do, but we can't take him with us."

Freeing Canary was a bad idea all the way around. He was too big to hide, and he couldn't be trusted not to "sing" and give them away. Jem listened. There was no sound of the donkey's brays. "We'll come back for him when Pa gets here."

"Can't we just cut him loose and let him run off?" Ellie asked.

Jem paused. "Maybe. But no promises. Now, come on. I think we've rested long enough. Look over there. We're getting close to the clearing and the creek."

A pale, silver light was shining up ahead. Either the stars were brighter than usual tonight, or a late moon had risen over the Sierras. Whatever the reason, Jem's heart began to beat faster. So far, he'd heard no sign of pursuit, but that could change in an instant. Once in the clearing, it would be hard to find a place to hide.

Jem pushed himself up from the ground and helped Ellie to her feet. Like sleepwalkers, they trudged along beside the flume. When they broke out into the open a few minutes later, Ellie gasped. The flume, the trees, and the clearing were lit up by a bright quarter-moon. "It's like a fairy land!" she exclaimed.

Hee-haw! Hee-haw! The sudden, frantic braying told Jem that Canary had heard Ellie's voice. *Hee-haw! Hee-haw!* The donkey sounded terrified. Each bray grew louder than the one before, until his singing pierced the night like a set of loud, rasping bagpipes.

Ellie covered her ears. "Stop it, Canary!"

Jem looked around in panic. There was no chance the miners could not hear *this* mountain canary's song. It would bring them running to find the reason. He looked at the dark, shadowy form of the donkey standing under the flume fifty feet away. "Maybe he'll shut up if we cut him loose. C'mon, hurry!" Together, they raced across the clearing. Canary loomed up in front of them.

But the donkey wanted nothing to do with his rescuers. It was clear that he was beyond accepting his friends' help. He had been tied up too long, with a heavy pack on his back and no food or water. His terror at the approaching humans, combined with his hunger and confusion, made his eyes roll back in his head until the whites showed. Braying loudly, Canary lashed out in the only way he knew how. His hind legs went up, and he drove his hooves into the flume's flimsy support.

Crack! The wooden pole snapped, sending the shoddy flume and its watery contents plummeting down on the mule and the kids.

-≼ CHAPTER 17 ≽-

Cold and Wet

Ellie screamed. She stood frozen in place, staring at the flume, clearly too frightened to move.

Jem was too scared *not* to act. He rushed at Ellie and gave her a desperate shove, which propelled her away from the worst of the falling debris. But Jem couldn't tell if she was out of danger or not. Water was drenching him in an icy flood. It streamed down his face, choking him, blinding him, until he didn't know which way to turn.

The flume was breaking up, crashing and thundering all around him. Jem dodged a falling plank and tried to cover his head. He slipped and fell to his knees, shaking with cold. Then a piece of the flume caught him across the shoulder blades and slammed him to the ground.

Jem lay in the mud, dazed. He hurt all over, but at least the runoff was no longer soaking him, and it was no longer raining splinters. The whole thing could not have lasted longer than fifteen seconds. He opened his eyes. One large section of the flume was gone. It lay in a heap of rubble close enough to touch. Water was spilling over the flume's far edge. It splashed down the hill and out of sight, back toward the creek where it belonged.

Out of the corner of his eye, he saw Canary. The donkey was in full flight, running and braying into the woods. A chunk of the flume's support bounced along beside him, still firmly attached by a rope. *At least he got away,* Jem thought sleepily. He felt content to simply lie still and thank God he was alive.

Then Jem heard another sound—crying. As the warm spring night slowly thawed his numbed mind, he tried to rise. "Ellie!" he called. Where was she? Had he pushed her out of danger? He fell back to the ground, pinned under the rubble. Twisting and shoving the boards away, Jem wriggled free and lurched to his feet. "Ellie!"

He picked his way around the wreckage, straining to find his sister in the moonlight. Her crying grew louder, and Jem finally stumbled on her. What he saw made him shudder. *Please, God! Let her be all right!*

Most of the flume fragments had missed her, but one of the supporting poles had not. It had fallen over, then rolled onto Ellie, trapping her under a torrent of water. She lay shivering in a shallow pool of flume runoff.

It was not a large pine pole, but it was long and looked solid. "I'll get you out of here in a jiffy," he promised. Jem took hold of the pole and lifted. It rose a few inches. He groaned. The log was heavier than he'd expected. Ignoring his own aches and injuries, he sucked in a deep breath and heaved it aside just enough to pull Ellie out of the water. When he reached down to lift her up, she threw her arms around his neck and nearly choked him. Even in the pale moonlight, he could see her face was scratched and swollen.

"I hurt," she whimpered. "I'm cold."

Thankfully, nothing was broken. But Ellie appeared in no mood to keep going. She sat down on the ground and wrapped her arms around her knees. Then she began to rock back and forth, crying quietly.

"Ellie," Jem said, dropping down beside her, "you know

Frenchy and his men must have heard the flume break up. There's no water in it now. They'll come looking for the reason, and they'll find us. We *have* to go."

No sooner had Jem spoken when his eye caught the twinkling of yellow lights in the distance. *Lanterns!* He jumped to his feet and lifted Ellie up to join him. "I'll help you, but we have to hide, and fast."

Ellie swiped a shaky hand across her face and let Jem half-drag her along. By the light of the moon, they stumbled down the rise and across the now-full creek above the falls. The mountain stream came up past Jem's knees, making him shiver all over again. He glanced behind his shoulder and saw the miners' lights gaining on them. They were following the flume, just as Jem and Ellie had.

Jem turned and headed for the forest. It was dark and dangerous, but he had no choice. The woods were their only refuge. By the time they plunged under the spreading branches, Jem was panting from pain and exhaustion. He wasn't picky about their hiding place. He shoved Ellie into a small stand of young pines and underbrush growing together and crawled in after her.

For a long time, they huddled there. Ellie couldn't seem to get warm. Her teeth chattered loudly and her whole body shook. Jem rubbed her back and her arms and held her close, but she couldn't stop shivering.

A sudden stream of curses jerked Jem nearly out of his skin. Frenchy and the others were getting closer, and they sounded furious. Jem covered Ellie's mouth and shrank deeper into the brush. He could feel her heart beating like a trapped rabbit's.

Jem watched the glow of the lanterns draw nearer. There was no place to run; no way to blend deeper into the brush. He could only hold Ellie tight to keep her quiet and hope his own chattering teeth did not give them away.

"When I find that boy, I will wring his neck," Frenchy muttered. "We should have thrown him in the hole right away, instead of tying him up." He cursed himself, Jem, and the miners.

"The kid didn't cut himself loose, DuBois," Jerky said. "He must've had help."

Another miner growled. "Could it have been the old man?"

Jem cowered and clenched his jaw. It felt like the men were closing in all around him. Ellie was crying soundlessly. He could feel her tears and shaking body through his hands. He tightened his hold and willed her to be silent.

"Not possible," Frenchy growled. "We dumped him far from here and left him for dead."

The lights moved in a wide circle, back the way they'd come, and the voices grew fainter.

"The boy'll bring the law right to our doorstep," Jerky said. "I say this operation's over. Let's pack up and get outta here before it's too late."

Three or four other voices muttered their agreement, and Frenchy swore again. He said something else, but the miners were too far away now for Jem to make out what they were saying. He let out a long, shuddering breath and held Ellie close.

They stayed like that until the swearing and arguing had faded into the night. Only then did Jem peek out of their hiding place and search the woods for lantern light. Nothing. Just black shadows against the pale light of the clearing.

With a sigh, he let Ellie loose, then slumped against a tree. "They're gone," he whispered, "but we're going to stay here the rest of the night. I'm too tired to go one more step, and I'm not taking any chances. Try to get some sleep."

"I can't," Ellie whispered. "I'm too cold, and my head hurts. And . . . I-I'm scared. What if they come back?"

"They won't," Jem said. *I hope not, anyway.* "Anyway, I'll stay awake and keep watch."

Ellie began sniffling again. "Tell me a story."

"A *story?* Now?"

"Please, Jem. Or some of those verses you got the prize for in Sunday school last fall. Anything, Jem. Anything at all. Just talk to me."

Jem searched his weary mind to come up with a story, but he wasn't good at making up tales about dragons and fairy princesses—stories Ellie loved. The only stories he knew came from the Bible or revolved around gold strikes, and Ellie knew those better than he did.

A chunk of Bible verses might be easier to recite.

"Jem . . ." Ellie said.

"I'm workin' on it." Finally, a few of Jem's favorite verses clicked into his memory. He started reeling off Psalm 27 in a husky whisper. "The Lord is my light and my salvation; whom shall I fear . . ." By the time he reached "though an host should encamp against me, my heart shall not fear . . ." Ellie had stopped shivering, and her breathing came soft and regular.

Jem made it through two more verses before he too drifted into a deep, dreamless sleep.

Cold, wet slobber on his face brought Jem awake with a startled gasp. He found himself lying flat on his back. Somehow he must have slipped to the ground during the night. Hanging over him, tongue lolling, Nugget's golden head blocked his view. He whined and licked Jem's cheek again.

Jem shoved the dog aside and scrambled to sit up. Bad mistake. Every muscle ached—his arms, his legs, his back, and especially his left shoulder. He'd banged it in the creek yesterday, and slamming into a tree last night hadn't done it any good. The flume falling on him had been the final insult. He could barely move.

Jem grimaced and scooted himself against the tree. His head felt full of wet cotton. He rubbed the sleep from his eyes and looked around. Sunlight was streaming through the foliage. Everything looked bright and cheerful. A few feet away, Ellie lay curled in a ball, sound asleep. Nugget reached across Jem's legs and gave Ellie a swipe of his tongue. She didn't twitch.

"Some watchman I am," he muttered. To his relief, Frenchy and his cohorts had not returned. Not even a night creature had interrupted their sleep.

"You found us," Jem said, ruffling Nugget's fur. He knew they might still be in danger, but the sunshine had revived Jem's spirits. "Shouldn't you be with Strike? Did you go off and leave him?" Nugget whined and thumped his tail. He looked pleased with himself for finding them. "Yes, you're a good—"

The dog bounded away through the trees and into the clearing. *Where's he off to now?* Jem wondered. No matter. It was time to get up and return to Strike. "Pa might be there this very minute!" He reached over and shook Ellie. "Wake up, Ellie. It's morning."

Ellie swatted at Jem's hand and rolled over. She curled up tighter, clearly not ready to begin the day. Old pine needles and dead grass stuck to her hair and covered her clothes. Jem shook her again. "Let's go. Strike needs us. Pa's on the way."

This time, his words penetrated Ellie's sleep. With a sudden lurch, she sat up and glanced around, eyes round and scared. Then she winced. "My head hurts."

Jem's eyebrows shot up at the sight of his sister's face. One whole side was swollen and bruised. A shallow cut, dark with dried blood, ran from her forehead to her cheek. "You don't look so good," he said.

Ellie managed a weak grin. "You look like you got thrown down a mine shaft."

Jem grinned back. "It sure feels like I did." He offered Ellie his hand. "Come on."

Suddenly, Nugget was back, tailing wagging and with a share of kisses for Ellie. She gave Nugget his due, then they worked their way through the thicket and stood up. Nugget ran ahead, but Jem and Ellie could not keep up. Limping and stumbling, they finally cleared the woods and broke out into the open.

A welcome sight met Jem's eyes. Cripple Creek tumbled over the falls like always. The broken flume stood useless, a short distance upstream. It was an ugly blemish on an otherwise beautiful morning.

"Well, kids, I'm mighty glad to see *you!*"

Jem's heart leaped to his throat. He whirled, expecting to see one of the claim jumpers pointing a pistol at him. His heart settled back into place at the sight of No-luck Casey, arms crossed over his chest, his bald head gleaming in the sunlight. *Doesn't that miner ever wear a hat?* It was a silly thought, considering all Jem had been through last night.

"Howdy, No-luck. We're mighty glad to see you too."

"Looks like you've had a rough time," Casey said, losing his grin. "We've been looking for you two for over an hour. Your pa's worried sick." He rubbed a hand over his head and shrugged. "Strike's pretty bad off, but we think he'll make it. Your cousin's with him now. That boy didn't do too bad," he admitted. "Not bad at all . . . for a greenhorn."

Jem sighed in relief. Nathan had come through. "Is Pa with them?" he asked.

Casey waved his hand toward the flume. "He and the others took off thataway to look for you. Not sure what's goin' on with the flume. It looks like a mess—"

"Did Strike warn Pa about Frenchy and the claim jumpers?" Ellie cut in.

"Frenchy?" Casey looked confused. "What about him?
He was banished weeks ago. Strike's out cold."

A sudden uneasiness prickled Jem's skin. If Pa had seen
the flume, he would of course follow it and see what was
going on. *But he doesn't know it's Frenchy!* He swallowed. "How
many came along with Pa?"

"Me and a couple others—Slim Barton and Dakota Joe."
Casey chuckled. "How many do you think it takes to haul one
old man back to town?"

"More than that," Jem muttered under his breath. He
and Ellie exchanged worried looks.

No-luck Casey stepped forward and lifted Ellie into his
arms. "It's a long way back, girl. You rest easy. I can carry
you." He motioned to Jem. "Come on."

"Frenchy's got half a dozen miners working a claim by
the flume," Jem burst out. "I've gotta find Pa and warn him
before he gets there."

Casey shook his head. "Listen here, young fella. You're
not goin' anywhere but back with me. The sheriff will . . ."

Jem took off running. Pa was outnumbered, and he was
walking straight into a hornets' nest.

CHAPTER 18

Badge of Honor

Jem sprinted toward the flume. His muscles screamed in protest, but he ignored the pain and splashed across the creek without slowing down. As before, the flume was an excellent trail marker through the woods, leading him straight back to Frenchy's claim.

He saw no sign of his father, Dakota, or Slim along the way. He stopped to catch his breath, rest his burning muscles, and consider his next move. If Ellie was able to get close to the claim without being seen, then so could he.

A cold, wet nose shoved its way into Jem's hand. He jumped. "Nugget! Go back."

Nugget looked up.

Jem didn't really expect his dog to obey. To be honest, he was glad for the company. "Just stay out of sight," he said as they slipped between the trees beyond the flume. It was easy to stay hidden. It became even easier when Jem reached the edge of the chewed-up claim. None of the miners were looking in his direction. Their attention was riveted on the three intruders standing in their midst.

Oh no! I'm too late! Jem sagged against a large pine tree a mere stone's throw from the men. Only the thick cover of trees and brush kept him from being discovered.

Nugget gave a low growl. Jem hushed him. Cautiously, he spread the branches apart and studied the camp. The miners had nearly finished packing. Another hour and they would have been long gone. A number of horses stood saddled; three burros were loaded with bundles nearly as large as they were. One of the donkeys looked like Canary. *They're stealing Strike's burro!*

A loud voice drew Jem's attention back to the reason he had come. Six miners surrounded Pa and the others, but only four of them appeared to be armed. Not that it mattered how many miners carried pistols. Pa and his companions were unarmed. Their revolvers lay on the ground a few feet in front of them.

Jem squeezed his eyes shut. "Oh, God," he whispered. "What should I do? What *can* I do?" Whatever he did, it would have to be soon. He strained to hear what the men were saying.

"Surely you didn't think you could hide all this forever," Pa said, sweeping his arm in a wide arc to take in the claim. He sounded calm as always. For all Jem could tell, he might be passing the time with Reverend Palmer after Sunday services. *How can he be so relaxed? I'm shaking!*

"We would have continued a lot longer, were it not for that boy of yours," Frenchy growled.

Pa's face turned hard. "Where is he? If you've done—"

"He might be down in that mine." Frenchy jerked his chin toward the dark opening in the ground. "You and your deputies"—he spat—"will be joining him soon."

"Jem!" Pa called toward the mining hole. "Are you down there?"

Frenchy laughed but kept his revolver steady. "I did not say he was down there alive, Sheriff." He motioned to his partners. "Get their weapons."

He's going to kill Pa! Jem's thoughts spun nearly out of

control. *I have to do something right now. Something to surprise them.* His gaze fell to the ground. Numerous stones lay scattered at his feet. He reached down and scooped up the first rock he touched. Unlike David and his five stones, Jem would only get one chance against *this* giant.

"Pretend you're striking out Will Sterling," Jem told himself, flexing his good arm. He steadied his shaking hand. *If I miss . . . No! I always strike Will out.* He stepped out from behind the brush, took aim, and—with all his might—hurled the rock fast and true.

Frenchy yelped when the rock slammed into his hand. His pistol went off with a loud *crack* and dropped to the ground. The shot went wild. Smoke billowed up into Frenchy's face. It gave the sheriff the split-second distraction he needed.

Jem watched, mouth agape, as his father dived for the weapons on the ground in front of him. Snatching up his revolver, Pa kneeled and got off one . . . two . . . three shots. Each round hit its mark faster than Jem could blink. The men howled in pain and astonishment, and clutched their arms. Their weapons fell to the ground, useless.

Jem lost sight of what happened next. A cloud of smoke from firing off the rounds of black powder swirled around Pa and the others in a thick, choking screen. But Jem heard no answering shots. He held his breath and waited. A blur of gold streaked by and disappeared into the smoke. When someone screamed, Jem knew Nugget had gone after one of the miners.

The smoke began to clear. Frenchy cursed and screamed at his partners. He dived for his pistol but froze when Pa cocked his revolver. "I wouldn't try that if I were you. I have a couple shots left, and I'm looking for a reason to use them."

Frenchy sagged in surrender and backed off, swearing under his breath.

"Keep a civil tongue in your head, DuBois," Pa ordered.

He whistled to the dog. Nugget trotted over to his side and sat down. He growled at Frenchy.

Jem didn't move. In less than ten horrifying seconds, his father had completely turned the tables on the miners. No wonder they seemed bewildered. Jem was so stunned he could hardly breathe. He swallowed. *How is that even possible? No one is that fast with a gun.* But his eyes told him a different story.

He suddenly remembered the fight in front of the saloon. Pa had knocked the knife out of Frenchy's hand with one shot. It hadn't dawned on Jem at the time that there might be more to his father becoming sheriff than Pa let on. A twinge of regret stabbed him. He had been wrong to worry and fret so much. It looked like Pa could take care of himself . . . and everybody else for that matter. Sudden admiration surged through him. *That's my pa who just did that!*

Before Jem could think of all the ways he'd been a fool lately, he heard Pa calling his name. "Is that you, Jem? You can come out now."

Jem stepped out from behind his cover and raced across the claim. He threw his arms around his father, laughing and crying at the same time. "Pa!" he said in a rush. "How didja do that? I've never seen such a thing!"

Pa squeezed him in a tight, one-armed hug but didn't reply.

Dakota chuckled from where he stood standing guard over the wounded miners. "Why, boy! Didn't you know your pa is the fastest gun in these parts? And he can shoot a button off a shirt. How do you think he got hired as sheriff?"

Jem's jaw dropped. He looked up into his father's face. Pa shrugged. "They sure didn't hire me for my good looks." Then he smiled at Jem. "That was a mighty fine piece of rock-pitching, Son. You gave me the distraction I needed. I'm proud of you. But . . . you've got a lot of explaining to do. Where's your sister?"

"She's with No-luck."

"Good." Pa released Jem and turned to Slim. "Find some sturdy rope and tie 'em up. It's a long way back to town."

"I say we tie 'em up, all right," Slim burst out angrily. "From their necks."

Dakota agreed. "I see a fine hanging tree right over there." He pointed to a large oak. "No sense botherin' the miners' court with this. We all know how they'd vote. Casey would agree too. Let's take care of these no-good polecats right now."

Jem swallowed. He had no desire to see a hanging today—or any day. He watched the faces of the captured miners turn chalk-white. They clearly did not want to see themselves hanged today either. What would his father do?

"We're taking them back to town," Pa said. "They're going to spend time in our new jail, then they'll have a real trial, with a real judge and jury. No miners' court."

"But, Matt!" Slim protested, "They jumped Dakota's claim, ain't that right, Dakota?"

The miner glowered at Frenchy. "Yes, it's mine. I filed on it months ago but had a dickens of a time gettin' any gold out of it." He glanced at the hole, the flume, and the sluice box, as if seeing them for the first time. "Any gold you took outta that hole is mine, DuBois."

"What gold?" Frenchy asked, staring blankly at Dakota. Then he added, "You are welcome to all the gold you find here." His mocking smile told the story: the gold was hidden, good as gone.

Slim twisted the bindings around Frenchy's wrists extra tight. "Why you lowdown, good for nothing—" He broke off and cuffed him soundly. "Claim jumpers and thieves, all of them! They even kidnapped your *son*, Sheriff. Not to mention nearly killing Strike." He pointed to a sorry-looking Canary tied up with the miners' packs. "And they

137

mule-napped Strike's beast. That's near the same as horse stealin'." He stood up. "We all know what happens to horse thieves in California."

"I say we save the state the expense and go right to the hangin'," Dakota added.

Pa nodded. "True, that's the way we did it . . . in the *past*. But it's not 1849 any longer. The lawless days of the gold rush are over. I was hired as sheriff to enforce the law." He pointed to the disheveled group of wounded, groaning men tied up on the ground. "And the law applies to them too. There'll be no more of this gold-camp justice, boys, or guilt by majority vote. A real judge and jury will decide if they hang or go to prison."

The two men deflated visibly.

"Whatever you say, Sheriff," Dakota muttered. "But San Quentin's too good for 'em."

Pa glared at Frenchy and the other miners. "I agree, but it's not up to us." He found a spare revolver and held it out to Jem. "Jeremiah Coulter, with an aim like you've got, I could use an extra deputy. We're slightly outnumbered. Can you help guard these men until we get back to town? The way they're feeling, they shouldn't give you any trouble."

Jem's hand shook—just a little—as he took the weapon from his father. After all, holding a gun on a group of men was a lot different than going after squirrels. He swallowed. Then he gripped the pistol's handle and looked up into Pa's eyes.

"Yes, sir!"

Pa knew the way home without having to follow Cripple Creek. Even so, it took most of the day to make their way back to Goldtown. Ellie and Nathan rode Copper, but the rest of the men—and Jem—walked.

All except Strike. Pa insisted that Frenchy and his un-injured partners take turns packing the prospector out on a hastily constructed litter. The rest were tied together and forced to stumble along, surrounded by the sheriff and his deputies. Jem hoped they didn't lose too much blood before they got back to town. The rags tying up their injuries didn't seem to be working very well.

"Don't worry, Jem," Pa assured him with a wink. "They're griping and swearing too much to be seriously injured. They just won't be using their shootin' arms for a while."

A long string of horses trailed behind the group, their lead rope wrapped tightly around Copper's saddle horn. Canary made known how much he disliked being dragged along at the end of the line. His loud and constant "singing" grated on everyone's nerves until Frenchy finally shouted, "Will no one shoot that beast and give us some peace?"

By evening, the ruffians were crowded into the tiny brick jail and Strike rested comfortably at the Coulter's ranch house. Jem sat by his bedside, heart pounding, while Doc Martin examined him. *Please let him be all right,* he prayed.

"Strike's 'bout as tough as an ol' buzzard," the doctor announced after stitching up the miner's head and splinting his broken arm. "Tell your pa he'll pull through. Keep him down for a week or so—if you can. Once he wakes up and finds himself under a roof, he'll be itchy to get out and back to his tent."

Jem chuckled. "He's not the only one itchy to have him out." Aunt Rose had been fluttering around the kitchen all evening, trying to be gracious yet clearly distressed at seeing the old prospector resting under the covers of her and Ellie's bed.

Doc Martin closed his black bag, snagged his hat, and turned to go. "I'll come by in the morning."

Then he was gone, leaving Jem and the unconscious

Strike alone. Jem looked down at his friend, grateful that he'd been found in time. He sat there a long time, thinking and reliving the last day and horrifying night. There was so much he wanted to say to Pa when he came home. Like how sorry he was for complaining about Pa's new job, and how proud he was that *his pa* was the sheriff of Goldtown. He wouldn't be embarrassed when the kids teased him about being a sheriff's kid either. *No, sir! Not anymore.* Jem grinned. *I wonder if Pa will teach me to shoot fast like that.*

He didn't notice the shadow in the doorway.

"You all right, Jeremiah?"

Jem looked up. Pa filled the door frame, tall and strong. He looked tired but satisfied with a job well done. Just then, Pa did not look like a rancher-turned-sheriff. Instead, he looked like the hero from Jem's favorite dime novel—riding to the rescue, dispensing law and order, tempering justice with mercy. Suddenly, the silver star on his father's vest did *not* look like a bull's-eye for outlaws.

It looked like a badge of honor.

Historical Note

Although Goldtown, California, is a fictional town, it blends elements from actual gold camps and towns that boomed (or busted) during the California Gold Rush of 1849–1864. It gives readers a glimpse into life in the gold country of the Sierra Nevada, where fortunes were made and lost, life was cheap, and prospecting was not for the faint of heart.

One essential aspect of life during this time was the miners' court. During the early years of the gold rush, thousands of gold-fevered men flocked to the camps. The lack of established laws allowed sinful human natures to run wild.

Eventually, the miners realized something had to be done. Each gold camp or district created a set of rules to protect the miners against claim jumping (stealing another miner's claim), murder, and other acts of lawlessness. When a miner broke the rules, a miners' court was assembled.

Court rooms did not exist. Folks were more interested in staking gold claims than building a courthouse. They held miners' courts wherever it was convenient—in a tent, a rough cabin, or even in a wickiup, a Native American shelter. In Goldtown, the miners' court was held in the saloon.

Before jails, only three punishments resulted from the miners' court: whipping, banishment, or hanging. The jury—a formal, twelve-man jury or a jury of the "whole" (the crowd)—decided on the punishment. Anyone could vote, whether he

141

or she had heard all of the evidence or not—even a passerby who happened to show up when the vote was being taken! They could even vote again. One story goes that in 1863, three men convicted of murder were sentenced to hang. They were on their way to their executions when some soft-hearted women and the defense attorney convinced the crowd to vote again—and again—until the men were banished instead of hanged. Later, one man returned to town and was hired as the deputy, even though an eyewitness had seen him shoot the victim! (He was hanged six months later for the crime, and justice was served.)

Traditional courtroom procedures eventually replaced miners' courts as rough gold camps grew into civilized towns with families, churches, schools, and businesses.

Visit www.GoldtownAdventures.com to download a free literature guide with enrichment activities for *Badge of Honor*.

About the Author

Susan K. Marlow is a twenty-year homeschooling veteran and the author of the Circle C Adventures and Circle C Beginnings series. She believes the best part about writing historical adventure is tramping around the actual sites. Although Susan owns a real gold pan, it hasn't seen much action. Panning for gold is a *lot* of hard work. She prefers to combine her love of teaching and her passion for writing by leading writing workshops and speaking at young author events.

FOLLOW JEM AND HIS SISTER, ELLIE!

**Twelve-year-old Jem stumbles into exciting
adventures in the Goldtown Adventures series**

*Badge of Honor • Tunnel of Gold
Canyon of Danger • River of Peril*